CERTAIN THREAT

BY KIMBERLY ROSE JOHNSON

Certain Threat
Published by Sweet Rose Press LLC
U.S.A.

All Scripture quotations, unless otherwise indicated, are taken from the Holy Bible, New International Version®, NIV®. Copyright ©1973, 1978, 1984, 2011 by Biblica, Inc.™ Used by permission of Zondervan. All rights reserved worldwide. www.zondervan.com The "NIV" and "New International Version" are trademarks registered in the United States Patent and Trademark Office by Biblica, Inc.™

ASIN B08C7BW7D8
ISBN: 978-0-9984315-9-8

Dedication

Dedicated to Uncle Kurt. Thanks for
all you've done to keep others safe.

Author Acknowledgments

As with most big things this book didn't happen by my sole efforts. I would like to thank those who had a hand in making this book what it is. Fay Lamb, thank you for your excellent editing skills. You always find ways to improve my stories. To my beta readers, your input is invaluable. I hope you enjoy the final product. To my proofreaders, thank you! Each of you has your own specialty when proofreading, which I appreciate so much.

Finally, to my Uncle Kurt, thanks for your valuable input and rescuing me from my own over creative mind.

1

Frank Davis ducked behind an alley dumpster while his client cowered behind him. At least they were out of view from the man who had been trailing them for the last three blocks. He sent a mayday text to his buddy, Dillon, on the Seattle police force, praying the man was not only working, but nearby.

Footsteps in the alley crept closer. Frank held his Glock at the ready. It was time to end this.

"I only want James," an angry, male said. "No one has to get hurt."

James' hand trembled on Frank's shoulder. "We're trapped," he whispered. "I can't believe you stupidly got us stuck here. Protection Inc. is supposed to be the best."

"Shh." Frank had regretted taking on this client almost from the moment he had signed the contract. They weren't trapped—at least not to his way of thinking—but James was correct. Things didn't look good right now.

Frank refused to accept defeat. He tuned out the insult. This had been his plan all along—ferret out the man who had been harassing James. After that he would enjoy what remained of his vacation next week and not be stuck protecting this rotten client. But leading him into a dead end hadn't been part of his strategy. He really needed to study a map of Seattle before pulling a stunt like this again.

Clipped footsteps sounded on the pavement, drawing closer.

"Don't move," Frank whispered. He peeked out from the side of the smelly dumpster and tightened his grip on his Glock. He rose, aiming his gun at the man who stood a little more than five feet tall.

"Whoa!" The man raised both hands. "You don't need that thing." His gaze focused on the Glock.

"Hands where I can see them," Frank ordered.

"Easy now." The man slowly raised both hands to mid-chest. "I have no issue with you. I only want that blood-sucking thief."

The accusation of theft didn't surprise Frank. He'd discovered belatedly that the financial planner was a less than upstanding person. "This isn't the way to get even. You can file a police report. Let the authorities investigate. Allow justice to run its course."

"He stole my money," the man shouted. "It's Christmas. What kind of person robs a man during the holidays?"

"He sounds like the Grinch."

"Hey!" James snapped. "I hired you to protect me from people like him, not insult me."

"People like him? You mean you stole from more than one person?" Frank kept his focus on the man, who stood less than six feet in front of him. A squad car stopped at the end of the alley. Good. His buddy had received his text.

Officer Dillon Brady got out of his cruiser, keeping the vehicle between him and the alley. "Is there a problem here?" he called out.

The man following them turned his back on Frank.

No weapon was tucked into his waistband. Frank lowered his Glock. "This man needs to file a police report."

"What's your problem?" James snapped. He stood and walked over to Frank and jabbed his finger into his chest.

Frank grabbed him by the wrist and twisted his arm behind his back. "I've had about enough of you." He nudged him forward. "It's time you face your accusers." He would never take on a client again without first doing a full background check on the person. Someone he trusted had referred James to Protection Inc. Since his schedule had been clear, other than planned time off—he'd taken him on, much to the frustration of his business partners.

"This is the end for you. I'll ruin you and your business." Venom practically oozed from James' mouth.

Officer Brady walked around the squad car. He

nodded at the man who'd followed them into the alley. "Who's this guy?"

"Good question. I'll let him explain. But I believe if you investigate James here, you'll discover he embezzled the man's money."

James tried to wrench free.

Frank held tighter. "Don't. Just. Don't."

At the end of what had proved to be a rotten Friday, Frank pulled into his garage. He got out of his car and noted Katrina had parked in front of her house across the street—odd. She usually pulled into her garage. Maybe she had plans to head back out. Too bad. He would have liked to have seen her tonight. He closed the garage door and stepped into his house, flicked the light on, and kicked off his sneakers. He padded to the front room off the entryway then plugged in the Christmas lights Carissa and Marc, his business partners, had insisted he needed on his front windows. He had to admit there was something soothing about the tiny white lights that framed the large picture window. The tension in his shoulders eased as he closed and locked the door behind him. Thank the Lord he wasn't a cop anymore and forced to deal with crooks like James every day. Turned out the FBI had been investigating his former client. At least justice would be served, and the man was out of his life.

Now all Frank wanted was a hot meal and his favorite recliner. He padded to the kitchen, rubbing his hands together. The roast Carissa taught him how to make in the crockpot smelled amazing.

Boom!

Frank ran to the front window and gasped. His neighbor's garage had been demolished and was engulfed in flames. He tugged on his sneakers, threw open the door and then ran across the street.

"Help." Katrina White shouted from under the commercial-style metal-shelving rack she kept in her kitchen. The pressure on her back made it difficult to breath. She should have listened when Frank suggested she secure it to the wall. "Someone help!" She had to get out of here. She pushed with all her strength, but the rack wouldn't budge.

Smoke floated into the room. Her pulse thrummed in her ears. Her house must be burning.

"Katrina, where are you?"

"Frank? I'm in the kitchen. Hurry! I'm trapped." She gasped out the last words as the smoke grew heavier.

A dark form rounded the corner. He stooped beside her. "I'm going to raise the shelf. Can you slide out?"

"I think so."

He lifted the unit. "Go."

She belly crawled out from under the burden. "Thanks."

"Let's get out of here." He turned toward the front.

"No." She gripped his arm and pointed to the door in the kitchen. "This way."

He nodded.

She grabbed her purse, which sat on the counter beside the kitchen door as they rushed outside.

Smoke billowed after them. "Come on," Frank said. "Let's get away from here in case it blows again." He coughed as they hustled out of the backyard and through the side yard to the front of her house. Sirens sounded in the distance and gradually got louder. He turned to face her and gripped her shoulders gently. He looked her over from head to toe.

She'd never been so happy to see anyone. "Thank you for rescuing me. I could've died in there." She shuddered. Had that been the point? Had the conversation she'd overheard in the breakroom a few days ago really been what she'd thought. Whoever had been in there must have known she'd heard, and they were trying to silence her.

Frank pulled a piece of pasta from her long blonde hair. "You have a cut on your forehead. Are you hurt anyplace else?"

"I hurt all over, but I'm alive, and that's what matters right now." She looked at her home. What a mess. Her garage was more than likely a total loss. "My house exploded."

"I know," he said, a gentleness to his voice. "Any idea why?"

She shook her head and winced. "My head hurts."

"No doubt." He cradled her cheek in his hand.

She leaned into his touch.

"Looks like you smacked the floor when the shelving unit fell on you."

An engine truck pulled to a stop near her house, and firefighters got to work. "Come on. We'll be out of the way at my place." He wrapped his warm hand around hers as they walked across the street to his driveway. An ambulance rounded the corner and stopped behind the fire trucks. He released her hand and waved to them.

Two medics approached. One carried a case.

"This is Katrina White. She was inside when her house exploded." He stepped away from her, allowing the medics to take over. She looked at her house as a medic attended to her forehead. Much of the home stood intact. Maybe there had been a gas leak. That would be a much better option than where her thoughts had originally gone. She shivered in the cold night air. Regardless of the cause, she couldn't stay there tonight or any time soon.

Frank rested his hands at his waist and looked at his neighbor and good friend with new eyes. Was she in some kind of trouble? Could the blast have been deliberate? He'd only lived here for the past year and hadn't gotten to know his other neighbors well since he worked constantly, but Katrina had wiggled herself into his life. He couldn't imagine someone doing this to her on purpose. She was one of the kindest people he knew.

At thirty-eight, she was romantically unattached, and worked at a bank. She'd moved in a month after he had and had asked for his help lifting a few things. Since then, he'd mowed her lawn whenever he was mowing his own, and she always invited him in for iced tea or coffee afterward. They'd had many pleasant talks in that time. He'd ask her out if he wasn't married to his job.

She appeared to be in good hands with the medics, so he marched over to the police car that had driven up a moment ago.

The officer got out and caught his eye. "This your house?"

"No." He motioned toward Katrina. "It's hers. I live across the street. Pulled her out of the place after the garage exploded."

He didn't appear surprised the house had exploded. Whoever had called it in probably mentioned it to the 9-1-1 operator.

"I'm Frank Davis. What do you think caused this?" He had a few thoughts but wondered if the guy would come to the same conclusion.

The twenty-something looked toward the house. "No clue. But there will be an investigation. Who are you again?"

8

Frank motioned toward his home. "I live across the street. The homeowner is a friend."

The officer nodded.

Frank eyed the burning home. "I'm thinking a gas explosion would have been bigger. The propane tank on her grill in the backyard was still intact when we escaped out the back door, so it wasn't that."

"You were inside the home when this happened?" His eyes widened.

Frank shook his head. "No. My neighbor was. She was trapped, and I helped her get out."

"Excuse me. I couldn't help but overhear what you told the police officer. What can you tell me about what happened?"

Frank turned and spotted a well known television news reporter. He wasn't a fan of the man's sloppy reporting. "Nothing. Excuse me." He strode over to the police officer who had walked a few feet away. "The homeowner will be at my place." Frank motioned toward his house. He turned and headed back to his driveway where Katrina sat with a blanket around her shoulders on the stone wall that framed his yard. "How're you feeling?"

"Other than being sore and somewhat terrified, I'm great." She nodded toward the reporter who was now talking to the police officer. "That man looks like a reporter I've seen on TV."

"He is." He eased down next to her, noting the medics were packing up. "You said you're terrified. Why? You're safe now."

"I could have died."

"But you didn't."

"True." She sucked in her bottom lip. "May I tell you something in confidence?"

"Of course."

"I think someone might have tried to kill me."

Shockwaves reverberated through Frank. "What makes you think that?"

"I heard something I wasn't supposed to hear."

2

Katrina's blood ran cold at her own words, but it was too late to snatch them back. It was one thing to think them, but to say them out loud made it real. She had been in denial for days, but it was impossible to refute what had happened to her home. This is what she got for eavesdropping. Clearly, someone besides her boss suspected she had overheard whatever those men were planning and wanted to shut her up.

Frank was a good man, and she trusted him, but what if telling him about that conversation put him in danger too? Not that she had much to go on or even knew for certain she was in danger. The explosion could have been her hot water tank or a natural gas explosion. Until she knew for sure the cause, there really was no way to know if she was in danger or not.

"What do you think you heard?"

She shook her head. "Forget I said anything. I'm sure the explosion was an accident." She couldn't risk Frank getting involved. She liked him and didn't want him hurt. As it was, he could have been killed while trying to rescue her, which went to show what kind of man he was. No. Telling him was a bad idea.

"Did you smell gas?"

She shook her head and winced as pain shot through it. She stilled and rested her gaze on the destruction. What was she going to do? She was alone in Seattle. No family within a hundred miles and no friends close enough to depend on, unless she counted Frank.

"Hey, whatever it is, I'd like to help. This is what I do."

"Help?" She glanced his way. She'd liked Frank from the moment they'd met. He'd been a fixture in her life. Funny, he was the only man she'd allowed to get even remotely close to her in over a decade. Not that it did any good. She'd still managed to walk into trouble. Her ex-husband's middle name had been trouble, and she'd learned to steer clear of men—most men.

If she hadn't forgotten her purse the other day at lunch and had to go back for it, she never would have overheard the mystery people talking. She blinked away the thought. Surely, she had misheard them. Besides, they had no idea she'd been listening, but Rick knew. Was he involved in whatever they were planning? Her boss wasn't her favorite person, but she couldn't imagine he'd rob their bank, or any bank for that matter.

"Yes. Please let me help, Katrina. As you know, I used to be a cop in Oregon. The rest of the story is, one of my business partners and I both quit the police force together and started Protection Inc. to help people like you. We brought in a third partner not long after we hung our shingle. We're good at what we do."

She chuckled. "You're confident."

"I back it up with results. I was about to have dinner. Join me, and we can figure out your next step."

She looked toward her home again. "Okay. I probably should eat something." Maybe a hot meal would help her to stop shaking. She stood and walked with Frank into his home. She paused in the entranceway. How was it she'd never been inside before?

The white marble-like tile in the entryway wasn't at all what she had expected. Frank seemed more the rustic-type than marble. The room directly to her left had white carpet and no furniture, unless you counted the Christmas lights in the window. She didn't. "You don't use that room? It's the perfect spot for a tree."

"Have you ever cleaned white carpet? Carissa tried to talk me into buying a tree too. When I first bought this place, I told myself my first project would be ripping up the entryway tiles along with that carpet and laying wood planks." He ran a hand along his neck. "I've been busy. I don't need that room anyway."

The scent of roast captured her attention. "Your dinner smells delicious."

"Thanks. Let's wash up and eat. I think we're both probably covered in an inch of dust and soot." He walked straight ahead and through a small doorway into an open-concept kitchen with an island that faced the family room. He washed up to his elbows in the sink.

"Ah, this is where the living takes place." Though sparse, it still felt homey. She needed homey right now. The space wrapped her in a warm hug.

"What gave it away?"

"The worn leather chair facing the big-screen television and the comfy-looking sofa." She motioned toward the family room.

He grinned as he removed a serving bowl from the cupboard. Then, using tongs, he took the veggies from the crockpot and placed them into the bowl.

She glanced down at her dusty clothes. "Is there someplace I can wash up?"

"There's a bathroom attached to the laundry room." He motioned toward a door, which must be where the bathroom was. "Or you can use the sink here."

She had no desire to be alone just yet. "This is fine. Thanks."

Frank pulled a platter from the cupboard and then removed the roast from a large crockpot.

"You don't have a table to eat at?" It had been a priority with her family growing up and one she'd carried into adulthood.

"There are stools at the island. It's rare that I get to eat here since work keeps me so busy. But I promised my employees and business partners we'd close up the office for two weeks at Christmas, so I find myself with some spare time. Thought I'd learn to cook over our break."

"Oh? Didn't I see you head out to work this morning?"

He dipped his chin. "You're observant. Today was our last official day of work before our break, but I wanted to get a jumpstart on cooking." He reached for two plates on an open shelf. "Figured I'd learn how to make a few holiday foods this next week. Mashed potatoes follow this roast in items I want to know how to make. I have the next two weeks off to learn."

She sighed. "I can't believe my house blew up a week before Christmas."

He frowned. "Now that you mention it, the timing is rude. But most of your house is intact, so it's not as bad as all that. You're probably only looking at water damage inside your house. Though your garage is a complete loss."

"I suppose, but the water damage makes it not habitable."

He pulled out his smart phone and pecked at the screen.

"What're you doing? I thought you were hungry."

"Carissa's tutorial said to let it rest on a plate. You're welcome to go for it though." He continued to type on his phone another minute and then set the device on the counter. "I'm sure it's fine." He pulled open a drawer and pulled out a carving knife. He cut off two generous slices and then put one on each plate. "Help yourself to the veggies."

She added carrots and a couple tiny potatoes to her plate. "You mentioned Carissa before. Is she your girlfriend?" He'd never mentioned one previously, but maybe this was something new.

He choked on whatever was in his mouth.

She rushed to the sink and filled a glass he had sitting beside it.

He took it from her and swallowed. "Thanks."

"I didn't mean to make you choke." But now she really wanted to know about this Carissa woman.

"You took me by surprise. If you knew her and saw us together, you never would have asked that question. I was Carissa's training officer then her partner for a while when we were cops. I moved up to detective and was assigned a new partner." He frowned and looked sad before he quickly schooled his face. "Carissa and I became business partners when we left the police force."

"Okay. But that doesn't really answer my question. You've mentioned her several times. She seems like someone who's more than a business partner."

"She has a boyfriend, so no, she's not my girlfriend. If I had to put a label other than what I've already stated, I'd say she's like a daughter to me."

Katrina hid a grin behind her napkin. "I'd love to meet her sometime."

"You'll get your wish soon. She and Marc, along with the rest of the team, are on their way over."

"What did you do?" She didn't want to involve all these people. "I thought everyone was on vacation."

He shrugged. "They didn't have to come."

"I have a feeling they'd do anything for you."

He took another bite. "This is pretty good for my first roast."

She waved her fork in the air. "Don't try and change the subject. You had no business involving your team in my situation."

He set down his fork. "You're right. What do you want me to do? I can call them off."

She hadn't expected him to give in so easily. If he'd been Jason, her ex-husband, he never would've relented. "Umm. Do you really think we need your entire team involved?"

He shrugged. "I don't know. You still haven't told me what you know. We also don't know the cause of the explosion." He took another bite, chewed, and swallowed. "It's your call, but you better decide fast. They're going to be here any minute."

"Fine. I would love to meet your team, even if they're wasting their time."

He stood and pulled a gallon-sized plastic bag from the freezer filled with cookies, opened the fridge, and pulled out two bottles of sparkling cider.

Her jaw hung open. She snapped it shut. "Do you always keep that kind of stuff on hand? Since you said you rarely eat at home, I imagined your fridge would be mostly empty."

"I've had the sparkling juice for months. It was on sale. As for the holiday cookies, they were a gift from Sally. You'll meet her soon."

The doorbell rang.

"While I answer that, will you grab a plate from the cupboard and put the cookies out? There are cups in the cupboard beside the fridge and several more bottles of juice." He stepped through the kitchen doorway at the end of the entryway.

Katrina got busy. What an insane night.

A multitude of voices mingled in the entryway. She hovered where she had a good view of the group. Should she join them? No. Frank put her to work for a reason. He probably wanted to talk about her to his team. What was she going to do? She didn't trust easily, but that wasn't the issue. She liked Frank, and if she was in trouble with people who wanted her dead, she didn't want to bring danger to his doorstep.

The doorbell rang again. Frank opened it and a police officer stood there. "It's for you, Katrina."

She exited the kitchen.

The officer at the door wore a grim expression.

Fear shot through her.

3

From the vantage point of Frank's entryway, Carissa Jones noted the pale face of the tall thirty-something woman standing in the doorway to Frank's kitchen. Her dishwater blonde hair hung in waves to her shoulders. She must be Katrina, Frank's neighbor who prompted the SOS he'd sent to the team.

The officer at the door cleared his throat as Katrina strode toward him. "Ma'am, you own the house across the street?"

She nodded.

Carissa watched her closely for any subterfuge. Clearly, Frank liked this woman, or he never would have pulled the team off vacation. Was she good enough for him?

"I told the fire marshal I'd let you know the fire is out." The officer removed his hat and gave her a short nod. "I'm sorry to inform you that the damage is extensive."

"But I thought only the garage was destroyed."

"The resulting fire caused a good deal of destruction to the main house and then there's the water damage."

"I see. I guess it's a really good thing Frank rescued me then. Any idea what caused the explosion?"

"That's still under investigation. I'm sorry, but you can't enter the property until the investigation is complete."

"I understand."

"How can you be reached when we know more?"

She told him her cell number. "Call anytime. If I don't answer, please leave a message."

"I'll make a note of that. Someone will be in touch."

She nodded.

The officer left and Frank locked up behind him.

"I'm Carissa. This is Marc, Peter, and Sally. We're really sorry about your house."

Katrina offered a weak smile. "Thank you all for coming, though I'm not sure why Frank brought you here." She laced her fingers together in front of her then turned and headed for the kitchen.

Carissa glanced at Frank. Why exactly had he sent for them? He'd yet to fill them in.

"There are goodies in the kitchen," Katrina said.

"Goodies?" Since when did Frank keep anything worth eating in his house? She sniffed the air. "You made roast." She'd given him a short tutorial on how to make one but never expected he'd actually follow through.

He grinned wide. "And you're just in time to have some." He led the team into the kitchen. They each parked on barstools while Frank and Katrina stood on the other side. "Anyone want dinner before dessert, or would you like to go right to dessert?"

"I recognize those cookies," Sally said.

"Come to think of it," Carissa said. "So do I. They were really good, Sally. Thanks again."

Sally beamed. "You're welcome. So, boss, what's going on?"

A grim look rested on Frank's face. "As you heard, there was an explosion at Katrina's house this evening."

"That kind of thing happens now and then." Marc picked up a sprinkle-covered cookie.

"True, but this was weird. Only the garage and a section of the house immediately connected to it were destroyed in the blast. The concussion of the explosion tipped a free-standing shelving unit onto Katrina, knocking and pinning her to the floor. Based on what the officer said, the damage grew after we escaped."

"We?" Carissa asked.

"Yes. When I heard the explosion and saw her car out in front, I went inside to find her."

"Good thing, too, by the sound of it." That would explain the bandage on the woman's forehead. "I hope you're okay," Carissa said.

Katrina touched the bandage and then lowered her hand. "I'll be fine, thanks."

Peter reached for a cookie in the shape of a candy cane. "Do you think someone tried to kill Katrina?"

"It's possible. She overheard something that might have caused this situation."

Peter raised a brow. "Something worth killing over?"

Frank's gaze rested on Katrina.

Katrina sighed. "I really don't want to involve anyone in my problem. If Frank's suspicion is correct, then you would all be in danger."

Carissa reached for a Christmas tree-shaped cookie. "It wouldn't be the first time. What'd you hear?" She hadn't expected Frank's friend to be so reticent.

Marc wrapped his hand over hers that rested in her lap and gave it a gentle squeeze—probably a warning not to volunteer them for protection duty. They were traveling to visit her family in Oregon next week for Christmas.

A vacant look filled Katrina's eyes as if she was in a dream-like state reliving whatever she'd heard. She shook her head. "No. It's Christmas, and I won't ruin it for all of you."

Frank set his cup down with a thud and juice splashed over the side. "Why don't you let us make that decision for ourselves?"

"Because once I tell you, you'll be stuck."

Frank met the eyes of each of the team members. "You heard the lady. If you don't want to be involved, now's the time to walk. No hard feelings. I realize Christmas is this coming Friday and this could very well ruin your plans."

Carissa glanced at Marc. Would he hate her if she agreed to stay? Frank was like a dad to her. She couldn't let him down, no matter the bad timing. "I'm in."

Marc sighed. "Me too."

Sally stood and brushed her hand through her short coffee-colored hair. "I'm sorry, but I need to sit this one out. I made a promise, and I must keep it. If it was any other week, you know I'd be there for you, boss." She grabbed her purse and left.

Peter stood slowly. "My flight out of SeaTac leaves in three hours. Jenna and I are joining her parents in the Caribbean for the holiday." His imploring gaze begged them to understand.

Carissa didn't blame him for wanting to spend Christmas with his girlfriend. Especially since a little birdie told her he planned to propose. Besides that, he wasn't invested in this company like the three of them. He was their employee. "Tell Jenna hi for us."

Peter moved to leave then hesitated. "I feel bad. If you get into trouble—"

"We won't call," Frank interrupted. "Go with our blessing. You deserve some downtime. Have fun."

Peter furrowed his brows. "I'll cancel. It doesn't feel right to leave the three of you."

Carissa shook her head. "Nope. We're the bosses, and you need to spend this time with Jenna and her family. It's too important. We've got this. Don't forget that before you and Sally came on, we managed as a trio." At least they did with occasional help from law enforcement friends. But he didn't need to know that.

"I did forget." Relief covered Peter's face. "Okay. Thanks. Merry Christmas and stay safe." He looked pointedly at Katrina. "All of you. If you need it, my home in Warm Beach is available. The key is under the mat at the back door."

Frank frowned. "Seriously? You leave a key out?"

Peter shrugged. "I realize it's not smart, but my housekeeper prefers I leave the key there so she doesn't have it on her own key ring. It's in the country, and no one's ever around. It'd be a nice place to lay low. It's at your disposal."

"Okay. Thanks," Frank said.

Carissa waited until the door clicked and then returned her attention to their new client.

Katrina took in a slow breath and let it out. "I work at a bank and had headed out for lunch at one o'clock when I remembered I'd forgotten my purse. We keep them locked in a cupboard located in the hall across from the branch manager's office and breakroom. Two men were having a hushed conversation in the breakroom. Their tone grabbed my attention, and I couldn't help eavesdropping."

"Go on, Katrina." Frank nodded.

"I can't be certain, but I think they were talking about robbing the bank. Or at least one of them might have been. It sounded like one man was trying to pay off another guy to look the other way."

Carissa blinked. "Wait. You're saying people you work with are planning to rob their own bank?" It wouldn't be the first time, but still, she had a hard time buying that scenario. "Do you think they could have been talking about something else? Perhaps one of them was caught embezzling funds."

Katrina gasped. "I hadn't thought of that. To be honest, one of my worst fears working at a bank is that it'll get robbed while I'm there. I guess my head went there first without considering other options."

"Then what you heard could have been completely innocent?" Marc asked.

"No way." Katrina shook her head. "They were definitely up to no good. One of the men said he didn't want to go to prison. So whatever was being planned was absolutely illegal." Katrina looked down and then back up and caught Carissa's gaze. "I think my boss might be involved. He confronted me when I was eavesdropping. I wasn't actually looking at the doors, and I'm not sure if he came from his office or from the breakroom. He might have been in there when he spotted me."

Frank blew out a breath. "Let's assume they think you heard more than you heard. Why blow up your garage? Why not bring you in on the deal? It feels like a stretch to me to think someone tried to harm you."

"Really?" Carissa and Katrina said in unison.

"Think about it," Frank said. "She has no idea who was in that room. So how would they even know she had overheard them?"

"Rick, the bank manager, saw me and confronted

me. Remember? I wouldn't put it past him to say something to them even if he isn't part of their scheme. He doesn't like me. Sometimes it feels like he's looking for a reason to get rid of me."

Marc rested his elbows on the counter. "Does anyone besides us know what you heard?"

"Just John, one of the security guards. I was concerned and didn't know what to do or who to trust. He was guarding the bank at the time of the conversation, so I'm positive he isn't involved. I suppose he could have mentioned it to the other regular guard."

Marc nodded. "Okay. Back to your boss. You said he doesn't like you and wants rid of you. You really think he'd try to kill you?"

Katrina quickly shook her head. "I didn't mean it like that. I meant he wants me out of the bank. He and I have had some arguments about…procedure."

"Explain," Frank said.

"Well, I deal with loans. Most often mortgage loans, but really, any kind of loan. He has some underhanded thoughts on how we should process those loans to benefit the bank. I refused to cooperate. My clients always come first."

Katrina raised a notch in Carissa's estimation. "Maybe you should find someplace else to work with better ethics."

"That's definitely on my to-do list after what happened today. Christmas is a horrible time to be job hunting."

Frank looked at Marc. "Do you still keep in touch with Kyle Richards?"

"Yes. He's assigned to the Seattle Field Office. White collar crime last I heard. Want me to loop him in?"

Frank nodded. "See if he knows anything about the bank where Katrina works."

Carissa wasn't overly fond of the FBI special agent since he'd tricked them when they'd hired him to help them protect a little girl in Oregon last summer, but Marc still thought highly of the man. Her feelings aside, they could use any intel he might have—not that he was good at sharing information, but it was worth a try. "How do you want to handle this, Frank? She can stay at my place, or we could all camp out here. Though it's lacking in Christmas spirit." She couldn't resist the dig. Teasing Frank was too much fun even under the current circumstances.

"For tonight, we'll all stay here, and not another word about my lack of décor."

She rolled her eyes, suppressing a grin so as to not aggravate him further. She liked to tease him, but maybe tonight wasn't the best timing.

With phone in hand, Marc walked into the front room. Her gaze followed his progress until he stepped out of sight. She blew out a breath. This case had definitely messed up their plans.

"Are the two of you a couple?" Katrina asked.

"Yes. We met on a case last summer after Frank hired him behind my back."

Katrina widened her eyes and focused on Frank. "I thought you were a team player."

He frowned. "I am. Our team was too small, and we needed the help."

"Pff," escaped from Carissa's lips before she could stop it.

Katrina chuckled.

Marc strode into the kitchen. "Kyle wants to talk to you, Katrina." He held out his phone.

Katrina reached for it with trembling fingers. "Hello?" She filled in the blanks she'd left out when she'd told them her story.

Carissa motioned to Frank and Marc to follow her to the front room. She kept her voice low. "What did he say?"

"Not much. He's taking her statement."

"He didn't tell you anything at all?" Carissa asked.

Marc shook his head.

Frank hooked a thumb into his belt loop. "It's times like this I miss being a cop."

"Why's that?" Carissa couldn't imagine how being tied down to proper procedure could help them.

"I want to get my hands on all the evidence that's processed."

"Then ask. I'm sure Dillon would be willing to help us out." Officer Brady had become a good friend to all of them, and unlike Kyle, he shared information.

Marc crossed his arms. "At this rate, we're going to need to add Dillon to our payroll."

28

Carissa shook her head. "It's not our fault he responds so often to our calls for help. Seems it's meant to be."

"What is?" Frank asked.

"Dillon working for us."

Frank shook his head. "No way. We need an inside source we can count on, but you did give me an idea."

Katrina walked into the room. "I'm sorry to interrupt." She handed Marc his phone. "He said to tell you not to be a stranger."

Marc pocketed his phone. "Be right back. My go-bag is in my pickup."

"Mine too." Carissa joined him. "So what do you think?" She tucked her hands inside her jacket pockets and walked beside him to their vehicles, which were parked a half block away since they couldn't get any closer due to the fire trucks.

"I'm not sure. I didn't want to say anything in front of Katrina, but Kyle's running a background check on her."

"He thinks she's lying?" Carissa popped the trunk on her car.

Marc unlocked the box in the bed of his pickup and pulled out his bag. "He'll let me know if he finds anything concerning. In the meantime, he said we're doing the right thing by being cautious. He suggested she use a sick day for work tomorrow if the bank is open on a Saturday."

"Agreed." She looked toward Katrina's house.

Eerie stillness settled around them. She shivered in the cold December air. "Want to check out the site?"

"And get arrested for trespassing or tampering with a crime scene? No, thanks." He waved a hand toward a squad car coming their direction.

"It's not a crime scene—yet." She had no plan to get arrested. Marc or no Marc, she had every intention of snooping around that mess. They walked hand in hand back to Frank's house. "Before we go in, are you sure you're okay with us working this case with Frank? I know how much you were looking forward to going with me to my parents'."

"I can think of several other ways I'd rather spend our vacation, but he needs us."

"Yeah. I think he might have a thing for his neighbor. Did you notice how his face softens whenever he looks at her?" She'd never seen him the way he'd been tonight. He always cared about their clients, but his attitude toward Katrina was different. This was personal for him.

Marc chuckled. "No. Can't say I pay that much attention. Just because he's giving up his time off, it doesn't mean he has a thing for her."

She shrugged. "Guess we'll see." She pushed the door open. Warm air enveloped her. "You want to sleep down here? Keep an ear and eye out for trouble?"

"Sure. Where will you be?"

Frank walked over to them. "She can stay in my office upstairs. It's right beside the guestroom and has a pullout bed." Worry etched lines in his forehead. "Katrina is upstairs taking a shower. I put sweats and a T-shirt out for her."

"Stop worrying, Frank. We'll take good care of your friend." She would also make sure Frank's girl had what she needed even if she had to go shopping.

"I know you will," Frank said. "There's something I didn't mention earlier because I thought of it while you were outside. Katrina normally parks her car in the garage. She had just arrived home and had gone into the kitchen when the explosion happened."

Marc rubbed the back of his neck. "You're saying if she'd followed her regular pattern she would've been inside the garage? The part of her home that was demolished."

"Exactly. At first, I wasn't onboard with the explosion being an attempt on her life, but the longer I process everything she's told us the more concerned I am. I think someone is trying to silence her."

Marc blew out a long slow breath. "If what you're suggesting is correct, they're going to come after her until they succeed."

"My exact thoughts." A grim look rested on Frank's face. "This isn't over."

4

Katrina stared at the ceiling of Frank's guestroom. It was still dark outside, but her body clock said to get up. Silence saturated the house. Was she the only one who got up at five in the morning to work out before starting her day? Based on the physiques of her protectors, she had to believe they knew their way around a gym. Maybe they'd take her to theirs since Frank had warned her against keeping to her normal routine. Then again, with the way her body felt this morning, she wouldn't be going to any gym soon.

She took her phone off the nightstand and checked for messages—only one from the police officer from last night. She read the text.

"As long as you stay away from the garage, you may go into your home to salvage what you can."

"Yes!" She kicked off the covers and rolled out of the toasty bed. "Brr." Maybe she should rethink the decision to get up. No. She needed to move.

A polite knock sounded.

She flipped on the light and opened the door. "Good morning, Carissa."

"Hi," she whispered. She held an armload of clothes—Katrina's clothes.

"How did you?" Her gaze slammed into Carissa's.

"It's best you don't know. I've washed and dried them."

"You must have been up for hours." How had she not heard her? More than that, though, why would Carissa do this for her?

"I had enough sleep. Get dressed. I made coffee. Marc is asleep in the front room, but I think the house would have to crash down around him to wake him up." She thrust the armload of laundry toward her.

Katrina winced.

"Oops. That was probably a poor choice of words. Sorry."

"It's fine. Thanks for rescuing my clothes. How bad is my place? I haven't been brave enough to look, but I did get a message that it's okay for me to rescue what I can from the mess."

"That's great. It's pretty bad though. Let's just say those clothes look a whole lot better now than they did before."

"Wow. Okay." She moved to shut the door then stopped. "How'd you know I was up?"

"I was going to drop these outside your door when I heard a floorboard creek. Now get dressed. I want to chat before the men wake up."

Katrina quickly changed into gray leggings and a long sleeve baby-blue tunic-style top. Thank goodness she'd been wearing her most comfortable pair of boots yesterday. She slipped into them then headed downstairs.

Carissa, sitting at the island, held a steaming mug between her hands. She smiled. "Prepare for bliss. I ran home and grabbed my coffee machine and favorite beans."

"Wow. You've been busy." She wasn't a coffee lover, but turning down a cup didn't feel right. "Thanks. Is there any creamer?"

"Creamer is in the fridge. Sugar is in the cupboard right next to it."

Katrina added creamer to a mug then poured the coffee. She avoided sugar as much as possible. She took a sip and felt her eyes widen. "This is actually really good." If all coffee tasted like this, she might take up drinking the brew. She took another sip, clutching the mug handle in a tight grip. She really needed to relax, but something about Carissa's demeanor this morning wouldn't allow it.

"I told you that it's good."

She stood on the kitchen side of the island facing Carissa. "What did you want to talk about?"

"You."

"Me?" she squeaked.

"Yes. Tell me everything."

She tilted her head to the side. "Why?"

"It's important to your case. I need to know everything there is to know about you."

"Maybe we should wait for Frank."

Carissa eyed her over the top of her mug.

She resisted squirming. This woman must have been a force to be reckoned with in interrogation. "Fine. I'm thirty-eight, single."

Carissa coughed and raised a brow.

"Sorry, divorced. But that was years ago."

"Every detail is important. Tell me about your ex. What was he like?"

"The man was trouble with a capital t. He got mixed up with any scheme that came his way. He was always looking to make a quick buck."

"Then why marry him?"

Katrina bristled at the implied accusation but decided to let it go. Carissa was trying to help. "At first, he was wonderful. Then he wasn't."

"Explain. What do you mean by he wasn't?" Carissa clearly didn't mess around.

"He was mean."

"Physically abusive?"

"No. Verbally. He was on some kind of power trip. He needed to know where I was and what I was doing at all times. I have no idea why he turned into such a control freak, but I suspected it had to do with some guys he got messed up with." She didn't care to dredge up these memories. "I don't see why this is important. That was a long time ago. He's out of my life."

"Okay." Carissa took a gulp of coffee. "Do you have any enemies? Someone who might want to hurt you?"

Katrina narrowed her eyes. "You don't think what happened is related to what I overheard, do you?"

"I don't know. If what you say is true, they have motive, but I question how they would know you heard them unless, like you suggested, Rick was in on it and told them you were listening."

Katrina looked down, staring into her mug. "Well, I did ask around to see if anyone knew who had been in the breakroom. It could have gotten back to them." She shrugged. "Like they say, hindsight is twenty-twenty. What I can't figure out is how they would know where I live."

"Your personnel file would have your address. The real question is, if this was planned, how did they know you always park in the garage and when you'd be home? What's to say you don't go to the gym after work or out with friends?"

"Oh, I see where you're going. Hmm." She hadn't thought of any of this. "I didn't notice anyone following me, but everyone at the bank knows I'm a homebody, so it would be a natural assumption that I'd go straight home after work. As far as parking in the garage, I do keep a garage door opener in my car that would be easy to see if someone looked."

Respect glowed in Carissa's green eyes. She stood and poured herself another cup. "I see why Frank likes you."

Katrina twittered. "You make it sound like he has feelings for me."

"You don't think he does?"

"Good morning." Frank walked into the room. His dark hair was damp and his beard freshly trimmed. He wore jeans and a long sleeved forest green Henley.

Carissa raised her mug to him.

He glared at his partner and padded to the fridge. "I make a mean ham and cheese omelet. Would you like one, Katrina?"

"That sounds delicious. Thank you." She held in a giggle. Clearly, he'd heard some of their conversation and wanted Carissa to know he didn't approve. The dynamic between Frank and Carissa was definitely what he'd claimed. Relief filled her. She would not ask herself why though. She couldn't go there right now. "Is there anything I can do to help?"

"How about you tell me where you found those clothes."

"These ole things? They were outside my bedroom door."

"Imagine that." He looked pointedly at Carissa.

"I couldn't sleep. I didn't hurt anything."

"If her house turns into a crime scene, you could have contaminated evidence."

Looking like a grumpy bear, Marc walked into the room. "What's all the ruckus about? Do you people realize what time it is?" He wrinkled his nose. "Coffee." He shook his head, padded over to Frank's big leather chair, and then clicked on the news.

Carissa's eyes twinkled. "He doesn't like the taste or smell of coffee, and it appears he's not a morning person."

"I can hear you," Marc groused.

"We know," Carissa said. "Why are you so cranky?"

"Someone was up half the night."

Carissa's lips formed an O. "I'm sorry, I didn't mean to wake you. I thought you were asleep."

Katrina's insides warmed. She missed this kind of banter. Her family had been close in her growing-up years, but after marrying a man her parents didn't approve of, they'd drifted apart. "Would you like some orange juice, Marc?" She'd spotted a jug of it in the fridge last night.

Marc stood. "I can get it." He walked over to the stove where Frank worked. "That looks delicious, Frank. I thought you didn't cook."

"I'm a work in progress." He glanced over his shoulder toward the ladies. "What did you discover at Katrina's place, Carissa?"

"Nothing I didn't already know. Make sure you call in sick today, Katrina. Aside from the fact it could be dangerous, you'll want to get your insurance company to see the damage. Once the authorities give the go-ahead, you'll need to scour through your home to see what can be salvaged."

"I don't work Saturdays, so that's not a problem." The weight of everything she had to deal with hung like a noose around her neck. She reminded herself to breathe and tackle one thing at a time.

Frank placed a plate with a magazine-worthy omelet in front of her. Somehow she'd manage to swallow it in spite of the rising panic sending butterflies darting around her stomach. "I predict you will be a gourmet chef before long."

He patted her shoulder. "You probably want to taste it first. I might have exaggerated when I bragged about my omelet-making prowess."

She took a tentative bite. The gooey cheese oozed out of the side of the egg. "It's delicious."

Frank blew out a breath. "Score one for me." He turned back to the stove.

As far as she was concerned, Frank had a perfect score. Especially since he'd saved her life, taken her in, and surrounded her with professionals who were there to keep her safe.

Terror had filled her when she couldn't get out from under the shelving unit. If he hadn't come along when he had, she could have suffered from smoke inhalation.

Who or what had been behind the explosion was the million-dollar question. No one had determined there had been a bomb, but everything in her said she was in danger.

5

Frank looked around his kitchen at the people who meant the most to him in the world. CJ, errr Carissa and Katrina seemed to have hit it off. Why else would she have risked getting caught pilfering through the damaged house? But he couldn't shake the words he'd heard Carissa say as he walked in the hall. He hadn't tried to hear their conversation, but it was impossible in the quiet of the house.

Carissa knew him well. Maybe better than he'd like. He cared for Katrina. They'd clicked almost from day one. He didn't mow his other neighbors' lawns, and he certainly didn't spend any precious off hours with them—only Katrina. He hadn't given his feelings for her much thought until now.

His phone rang. He pulled it out and checked the caller ID. "Hey, Dillon. What have you found out?" Frank put him on speaker since Marc and Katrina were across the street seeing what could be salvaged, and Carissa was upstairs in the shower.

"The official word on the explosion is that it was a natural gas leak."

"You're kidding."

He rubbed the back of his neck. Could this entire thing have been one huge accident? Maybe Katrina wasn't in any danger after all.

"Nope. That's good news for your friend. I know you were concerned."

"I was. Thanks for the update. If anything new pops up with you let me know?"

"Sure thing. Have a Merry Christmas if I don't see you before then." Dillon chuckled. "Forget I said that. I know better than to think a week could go by without me being called to rescue you or someone on your team."

"Ha!" Frank said. "You make it sound like we get into trouble on a daily basis."

"Feels that way sometimes."

"Well, you can rest easy. We have the next two weeks off."

"Right. I'll believe that when I see it. You, my friend, are what they call a workaholic."

Frank gripped the phone tighter. He didn't want that word applied to him. "I know how to take time off. I took two weeks off at the end of the summer."

"I'm impressed. I gotta go. Stay safe."

Frank pocketed his phone. "That was not what I expected."

Carissa walked into the kitchen. "What wasn't what you expected?"

He rubbed his stubble-covered chin. "A gas leak caused the explosion."

"How? No one was in the garage to set off a spark."

"Good question. I'm not sure we'll ever know the answer to that question, but it appears no one tried to kill Katrina, and we might have actually put her in danger by having her give a statement to the FBI should they question her co-workers about what she overheard."

Carissa frowned and lowered her gaze.

He understood her silence. He'd been so certain someone was out to harm his neighbor, he hadn't bothered to seriously entertain the idea it was truly an accident.

"They're positive it was a gas leak and not a bomb?" Doubt filled Carissa's eyes.

"Yes. I'm sorry for dragging you into this. You and Marc might as well take off. You have time to salvage your plans."

"Not so fast. I'm not convinced she's not in danger. If what she says is true about what she heard, at the very least, something could be going down at the bank where she works. They might not have blown up her house, but they are definitely up to something. As long as I've known you, Frank, your instincts have been spot on."

"Thanks, but I think I was wrong this time."

"I'm not convinced."

"Convinced or not, it doesn't change the fact no one tried to kill her."

"Are you sure about that? Someone easily could have made it look like an accident. What if the line was sabotaged?"

"Say you're right," Frank said. "How would the perpetrator have known it would have exploded when she was inside? There are too many variables."

"Perhaps. Or the perpetrator was nearby, watching for her. Maybe he thought the house would go up when she opened the garage."

"She wouldn't have been in the garage. As soon as the door began to move, it could've set off the explosion. I open my garage door up a couple houses away from home." As much as he appreciated Carissa's faith in his gut, he wanted to be wrong this time. He'd much rather Katrina didn't have a killer after her.

"Hmm. I hadn't thought of that. What's our next move?"

"Your next move is to take some time off and enjoy yourself. Sleep in, read a book. I don't care so long as you come back to the office on the Monday after New Year's ready to work."

She wagged a finger at him. "I will so long as you promise to do the same."

He shrugged. "We'll see. I plan to help Katrina relocate until her house is repaired."

She tilted her head to the side. "What's with the two of you anyway?"

"She's a friend." A friend he cared for very much.

"You sure that's it?" Carissa didn't look convinced.

"Yes. Let's go tell her the good news."

"I'll be over in a minute. I need to grab my bag from your office."

He walked outside and spotted Katrina standing beside her car in the street. The roar of a fast-moving engine drew his attention. A white sports car raced toward Katrina. "Watch out!" he shouted and darted across the street. He hooked an arm around her waist, propelling them over the hood and onto the sidewalk. He stood and pulled her toward the house right as the car veered slightly to avoid hitting her car.

Katrina looked at him with confusion on her face. "That was close." She rubbed her elbow.

"Are you hurt?" He was sure his own body would have a few new bruises from that maneuver.

Marc ran toward them. "Are the two of you okay? That car looked like it was gunning for you. Or the driver was distracted and being reckless."

Frank set his jaw. He didn't care what the investigator wrote in his report. Someone was out to kill Katrina. He didn't buy it for one second that the person behind the wheel had been a distracted driver. He still had his hand wrapped around hers and realized she was trembling. Everything in him wanted to tuck her close. Instead, he released her hand. He couldn't think clearly if he allowed himself to get too close to her. "We need to get you away from here."

Wide-eyed, she nodded. "Where will I go?"

He had no idea. "We'll figure it out. Hurry up and

get what you need from your house. While you and Marc do that, Carissa and I will figure out a game plan." He sounded much more confident than he felt. He turned and strode across the street to his house.

Carissa stood in the driveway with her phone to her ear. "Thanks." She ended the call. "I missed the plate but called in the make and model."

"Good. I didn't know you were outside."

"I wasn't. I heard you shout and ran out here."

"We need to figure out where to move Katrina. She's not safe here. Let's go inside where it's warm." Cold had seeped through his jacket in the short time he'd been outside.

Carissa turned and walked beside him. "I told you you're always right."

"This was one time I wouldn't have minded being wrong." Peter's offer to use his home up north jumped into his mind as the perfect solution to their problem. "We should move Katrina to Peter's house in Warm Beach. She should be safe there." Were the mystery men at the bank behind this, or was something else going on that they didn't know about? He needed to have a serious talk with Katrina and then with Special Agent Kyle Richards.

Katrina bit down on her bottom lip to keep it from trembling as she stared at her packed car from the safety of the sidewalk. Considering the impact of Frank's body hurtling them across the hood, she only noticed one tiny dent. She could live with that. Frank had saved her twice now. She owed him big time.

Marc strode toward her. He carried the last box of stuff she'd managed to salvage. "This is it. Is there room?" He looked skeptically through the passenger-side back window.

"Yes." She pulled open the door. "I should have asked Frank if I could store this stuff in his garage, considering I have no idea where I'll be living until my home is okay to live in again."

He looked across the street and hesitated. "That's actually a really good idea. Let's store it here for now though. We can move it into the garage later." He placed the box in the only possible spot it could fit. "Let's get you inside before more trouble comes." He rushed her across the street and into Frank's house.

Frank sat in his leather recliner wearing a faraway look.

She cleared her throat.

He blinked and turned his gaze toward them. "Good. You're back. We need to talk." He stood, walked to the island, and pulled out a chair for her.

Butterflies visited her stomach for the second time in as many days. She didn't remember being nervous around Frank before, but things had changed. "What's up?"

"What's up is I need to know everything there is to

know about you. For starters, do you have any enemies?"

"No." Unless her ex-husband counted. They weren't exactly friendly. Thankfully, she hadn't had contact with him in years.

Frank narrowed his brown eyes. "But there's someone that came to mind when I asked."

Her face heated. "My ex-husband is the closest person I have to an enemy. But he wouldn't be behind this."

"Why not?"

"For starters, he doesn't know where I live. Then there's no motive. Why would he do any of this?" She raised her hands, palms up. "We might not have split cordially, but that was a long time ago. He's never bothered me since the divorce." Except for that time a couple of years ago. She ignored the thought. No one ever proved it was Jason who had vandalized her garage the day she had forgotten to close the door.

"Just the same, I want to look into him." He held a pen poised over a pad. "What's his name?"

"Jason Gibson. I went back to my maiden name after the divorce." She rattled off his date of birth and social security number. How did she still have that memorized?

"Okay. This is good. I'll do a little digging and see what I can find out, and more importantly, if he was anywhere near here yesterday or today. Does anyone else come to mind?"

She shook her head. "Are you sure the people at the bank aren't behind this?"

"No, but we're being thorough. If you're agreeable, we'd like to move to Peter's house up in Warm Beach. It's in an out-of-the-way location, and I think you'd be safer there than here. You can park your car in my garage, and we'll take my SUV."

"Okay." If she couldn't be home, it didn't really matter where she was, so long as she was safe. She shivered at the thought of what could have happened if Frank hadn't propelled her off the street when he did. She couldn't accept that Jason was trying to kill her, but who hated her so much they wanted her dead?

6

Carissa sat beside Marc in his pickup as he drove along a country road. It would take a chainsaw to cut through the tension. "Do you regret offering to help Frank?"

"No. But I'm disappointed."

"How so?"

"I was excited about going to your parents' home. Protecting Katrina messed up my plans. Then again, I should have expected something like this would happen. That seems to be how things go at Protection Inc. I make a plan and work gets in the way."

Her stomach dropped. "What are you saying?"

"Guess I'm in a funk. I'd been looking forward to our time off together. You know I love you, Carissa, and because of that, I'd like us to be more than the sum total of our business partnership."

"We are." They'd had a similar conversation a couple of months ago. "Just because our lives are consumed by work, it doesn't mean there can't be an us."

"I hear you, but sometimes I feel like so long as we are both part owners of Protection Inc., we'll never have more than a day here and a day there to ourselves."

She sighed, knowing the truth of his words. "What do you suggest?"

"Maybe I should step aside."

"From Protection Inc.?"

"Yes. I can't believe I'm even thinking that way. It sure wasn't in my head before."

"What would you do? Even if only one of us is employed there, time would still be a problem. This isn't exactly a nine-to-five kind of career." She couldn't believe he would consider leaving the team either. They were like family and needed each other. She had grown to depend on him and enjoyed working with him.

Had she made a mistake allowing him beyond her wall? She didn't see this turning out well for either of them. She should have listened to Frank's warning this past summer. Now it was too late. It felt like she was destined to have her heart broken one way or another.

"I don't know. All I know is this could be my last case with our company. I need more than work in my life, yet at the same time, I like how we make a difference in the lives of our clients. I love my job, but I need balance."

Her pulse thrummed in her ears. "Balance is good. I think we could work on that." He was right. They all needed to find balance. Their company consumed all of their lives, and it didn't need to be that way.

"Do you really think we could achieve that with the kind of work we do?" Marc signaled and pulled onto a gravel driveway that looked to be about the length of a football field.

"As the saying goes, where there's a will, there's a way. We need to get firm with Frank and demand changes."

He nodded. "Peter said his housekeeper put the key under the backdoor mat, right?"

The ranch-style house at the end of the drive was nestled between tall fir trees. "Yes. I'm sure glad he has this place. No one should connect Katrina to Peter's house."

"I agree. It's the perfect safehouse." He stopped in front of the single-level home. "I'll go retrieve the key."

"I'll get our stuff," Carissa said. "I wonder how we beat Frank and Katrina?"

Marc looked in the direction they'd come from. "I'm sure they'll show up any minute." He strode toward the back of the house.

Carissa shouldered her duffle bag and wrapped her arm around her coffee machine. The guys had made fun of her for bringing it along, but they wouldn't want to be around her if she had to drink inferior coffee for the length of this job, especially after the conversation she'd just had with Marc. They should give her credit for leaving her commercial-grade espresso machine at home. She'd had Frank cart it all the way to Oregon once for an extended job.

Marc opened the front door and strode outside. "It's not a mansion, but it's clean and warm inside."

"Works for me." She walked past him.

"Hey," Marc said gently.

She turned toward him.

"We'll figure us out." He gave her shoulder a gentle squeeze.

She nodded and headed for what looked to be the kitchen. One way or another, she wouldn't let her emotions get in the way of working with Marc. She had to trust the Lord knew what was best for both of them and leave it in His capable hands.

She placed her coffee machine on the kitchen counter then made her way to the first bedroom on the right—the master had a king-sized bed. Should she leave it for Marc and Frank or make it the girls' room? She meandered into the large space and spotted an attached bath.

"You taking this room?" Marc stood in the doorway.

"I'm considering it. It's only a two bedroom right?"

He nodded then crossed the hall to the other bedroom. "There's only a double bed in here. Guess one of us will be on the couch. That's probably for the best. As I recall, Frank snores."

Her phone vibrated. She slid her finger across the screen. "Where are you, Frank?"

"We made a slight detour. By the way, you're on speaker, and Katrina's with me."

"Okay." She appreciated the warning, though, where else would Katrina be?

"Remember Kratt Paper?"

"Of course." She'd never forget the paper company accused of polluting the Puget Sound.

"I just heard from the investigator I hired to look into them," Frank said.

"For real? Why didn't you do it yourself?" She knew he had strong suspicions about that company thanks to a former client's claim stating they were polluting, but she never expected him to put his own money on the line.

"With what time? The point is, they're going down. I sent everything I discovered to Dillon, and he's getting a warrant as we speak."

"I guess what's important is that they're going to be held accountable, not that you didn't find the proof yourself." Marc clearly was on to something when he spoke of balance. They should have time for pet projects and not have to hire them out.

"Yeah. I'm glad justice will be served."

"Thanks to you, my friend. Without your money financing the investigation, they would have continued getting away with polluting the Sound."

"And get this. It's bigger than the paper company. It extends to an inspector who looked the other way while the Sound was polluted."

Carissa sighed.

"You okay?"

"I'm fine. When will you arrive?"

"Soon. What's going on?"

"I don't want to talk about it right now." She sat on the edge of the bed. "See you when you get here. Did you stop for groceries?" That had to be why he was taking so long to get here.

"Yes."

"I hope you like vegetables," Katrina said. "I'm making vegetable and bean soup for dinner."

"Sounds good. See you soon." She ended the call then quickly unpacked her bag. Maybe if her clothes hung in the closet, Frank wouldn't veto her and make her switch bedrooms.

A short time later, the doorbell rang. Marc took care of letting Frank and Katrina inside.

"Knock. Knock," Katrina said a moment later. "I heard this is the girls' room." Her arms were laden with the clothes Carissa had salvaged along with a tote bag.

"You heard correctly. There's more than enough room in the closet and dresser. I'll let you get settled." She moved toward the door then stopped. "Do you mind sharing the bed? It's huge, so I assumed it'd be fine, but if you'd rather have a bed to yourself, the room across the hall has a double and the men could take this room."

"Isn't that the only other room?"

Carissa nodded. "One of the guys will sleep on the couch."

"This room works." Concern filled her eyes. "I

know you told Frank you didn't want to talk about whatever's bothering you, but if you ever need an ear, I'm available. It seems I have all the time in the world. Or at least until I need to return to work on Monday.

Carissa glanced toward the open door then back at her client. "Thanks. I appreciate the offer, but I'm okay." She left and found Frank in the kitchen putting groceries away. "What'd you get for us?"

"Mostly the basics, but Katrina insisted on baking Christmas cookies for everyone." He pulled out baking soda, salt, flour, baking powder, butter and everything else one needed for baking.

"That's a lot."

"I remembered Peter mentioned once before he didn't keep many food staples here."

"Guess that explains why there're so many bags." She reached into one and pulled out a tub of chocolate ice cream. She raised a brow. "Necessities?"

"Katrina wanted that too."

"Likely story," she teased. "This is way too much food for two nights. Katrina plans to return to work on Monday."

"We'll see about that. I'm trying to convince her to explain to her boss what happened and request the week off."

"Based on what she said about him not liking her, I doubt he'd go for it."

Frank shrugged. "Maybe not, but it's worth asking. It's much easier to lay low here while Dillon looks into her co-workers."

"I didn't realize he was going to do that?"

"Since Kyle didn't seem all that interested in the case, I gave Dillon a call."

Carissa nodded. "Kyle is so secretive, he could be investigating what she told him and keeping it to himself."

"Not sharing information is the problem. We need someone willing to keep us in the loop. Dillon agreed."

"Good." She glanced toward the hall that led to the bedrooms. "There's something you need to know." She lowered her voice. "Marc is considering leaving Protection Inc. after this case ends."

"What!" Frank roared.

Carissa flinched and put a finger to her lip. "Will you please keep it down?"

"I knew something was wrong, but I had no idea it was so bad."

Marc stood a few feet away. "Sounds like she told you."

"Yes." Frank's brow furrowed. "Are you sure about this?"

"No, but if we could go on as if nothing has changed, I'd appreciate it."

"Nothing?" Carissa asked. "I thought you wanted us to find balance. I really think you're on to something with that."

Frank frowned. "What do you mean by balance?"

"The three of us need to restructure the company so we aren't working twenty-four seven," Carissa said.

"We don't." Frank folded one of the paper bags the groceries had been in.

Why couldn't he see what was so blatantly obvious to everyone else? "Not literally, but we might as well be. You were too busy to investigate a passion project. If we had personal time built into our business, it would have been possible for you to handle that yourself."

Frank frowned. "I don't want to lose you, Marc. You complete this partnership, and we need you. What do we have to do for you to stay?"

Marc crossed his arms and propped a hip against the wall. "I suppose my biggest issue is that Carissa and I rarely have time together outside of work."

"You do realize many couples have this issue, and they make it work?" Frank rubbed the back of his neck.

"Yes, and that's great for them, but it's not working for me."

"Frank," Carissa said. "I appreciate how accommodating you've tried to be in the past, but I think the main issue is none of us knows how to say no to someone in need of our services. If we were more selective and had someone we could refer people to, I think we would feel better about turning potential clients away, and it would enable us to work weekends on a rotating basis."

"How would a rotation work?" Frank's probing eyes met hers.

"It will take exceptional organization for sure. If one of us takes charge on weekends then that frees up the other two on their off weekends. We'd have to bring in Sally or Peter and perhaps hire someone else like we've talked about for the past several months. I realize our profits will go down, but I think it's worth the sacrifice."

Frank glanced at Marc. "Would that work for you? It'd give the two of you one out of every three weekends together."

Marc lowered his arms and tucked a hand into his jeans pocket. "It's definitely a step in the right direction."

"Umm, excuse me," Katrina said. "I didn't mean to walk in on a meeting, but I think I have a problem." She held up her phone screen facing them.

Carissa moved closer and read the screen. "It's a news report about Katrina's home."

"Why's that a problem?" Frank asked.

"I'm mentioned by name in the story."

Marc reached for the phone. "May I?"

Katrina released it.

Marc's brow furrowed. "Homeowner Katrina White was reported missing by her ex-husband." Marc looked up from the device. "I thought you didn't have contact with one another. Why would he think you're missing?"

"We don't. I have no idea why he'd report me missing or why he's talking to the media. It doesn't make any sense. I haven't seen him or heard from him for at least a decade." She sighed. "Although I did wonder when my garage was vandalized a couple of years ago if he had anything to do with it."

Carissa's shoulders tightened. "How would he know you're missing unless he went to your home looking for you? Does he have your number?"

"No, he doesn't, and I don't know his." Katrina bit down on her bottom lip. Her brows furrowed. Then her eyes shot open wide.

"What?" Frank asked.

"How do we know the reporter actually spoke to Jason? Anyone could have called claiming to be him, hoping to find out information. This is the same reporter who covered the explosion, so it stands to reason someone seeking information about me would contact him."

Carissa nodded. "I see where you're going with this. I'll contact the reporter to see if he confirmed who he spoke to."

Marc pulled out his phone. "And I'll see if a missing person report was actually filed and, if so, by whom."

Carissa noted the frustration on Frank's face. "How about if you and Katrina make those Christmas cookies you talked about, while we make some calls?" Carissa stepped away and found a quiet place in a room with a floor-to-ceiling bookcase filled with books. "Whoa." It even had a wall-mounted ladder that ran on a track. "Cool." She sat on the window seat and got to work. One way or another, they'd get to the bottom of that news story.

7

The radio on the kitchen counter belted out a new-to-him Christmas tune. Frank much preferred traditional songs, but this catchy tune wasn't bad. Katrina hummed along to the melody as she scoured the cupboards for cookie cutters. The sugar cookie dough on the counter tempted Frank to eat it raw. It was a favorite growing up, but he'd learned self-control since childhood. Instead, he grasped the rolling pin and rolled the dough out on a marble cutting board. His team had vacated the kitchen nearly three hours ago and hadn't returned. What were they up to? It didn't take that long to answer the questions they had.

"I found cookie cutters." Katrina pulled a clear plastic container with a lid from a lower cupboard. She stood, a huge smile on her face, and held up her find.

"You mean I don't get to carve out shapes freehand?" He winked.

She grinned. "I'd like to see you try, but to be safe, we have these."

Frank looked around the cookie-cluttered kitchen. "I've never seen so many cookies all in one place except in a bakery." Katrina had made snickerdoodles while the sugar cookie dough hardened in the fridge. Then she'd made what she called a chocolate crinkle cookie. She mentioned wanting to make another kind too, but he talked her out of it, pointing out they wouldn't be able to protect her if they were all in a sugar coma.

"When I was a girl, my mom and I would spend the weekend before Christmas baking cookies. Then we would put them in decorative boxes and deliver them to our neighbors. It felt nice to do something normal today. Thank you. I'm sure you would rather have been doing something different."

"Not a chance. I've had fun." Surprisingly, he meant those words. This afternoon had been the most fun he'd had in some time. Relaxing too. "I'm glad we could recreate a good memory." He savored the glow of happiness in eyes that had been filled with fear since her house had been destroyed last night.

"I miss those simpler times."

He weighed his next words carefully. "What changed? I mean besides part of your house blowing up?"

She sighed and sadness crept into her eyes. "I married a man my parents didn't approve of. They wanted nothing to do with me after that."

"I'm sorry." To be rejected by your parents had to hurt. His own had passed years ago, but they'd always had a solid relationship. "Even after the divorce they didn't accept you?"

She shook her head. "How's that dough coming? You ready to start cutting it?"

"Sure."

Carissa poked her head around the corner and motioned for him to follow her.

"Think I'll leave the cookie cutting to you for now. I need to talk with my team."

Her eyes widened. "Oh. Okay."

He didn't like bringing her back to reality, but they were here for a reason—to figure out who was trying to kill Katrina and keep her safe in the process. He followed Carissa to a room filled with books. "What did you find out?"

"The reporter didn't confirm who he was speaking with over the phone."

"So it could have been anyone." For one of the few times in his life, he didn't know what to do. "Where's Marc?"

"He went to Seattle to meet with Dillon."

"How did I miss him leaving?" His brow puckered.

Carissa chuckled. "I'll give you one guess, and her name begins with a K."

"Cute."

"Dillon didn't want to talk over the phone and insisted on meeting in person."

"You think he knows something?" Hope sprung inside Frank for the first time this weekend.

"It's possible, but it's curious that he wanted to meet in person."

"Agreed. I wonder why he's being so cautious. What about Kyle? Have we heard from him?" Their FBI contact should have learned something about Katrina by now.

"That's where this gets really interesting. Marc got a text from Kyle as he was headed out for Seattle. Kyle has something to tell him, but he wanted to meet in person too."

"Why didn't you go with him?"

"And leave you here alone to face any trouble that could arise? You should know better than to even ask that." Carissa shook her head. "I don't know if it's Christmas or Katrina that has your head working at half speed, but you better get it together."

He glared at Carissa, hating that she was right. He was no good to anyone if he didn't keep his focus. He cared too much about Katrina, which made this personal—not something he was used to.

Carissa's phone buzzed in her hand. She looked down and read the message. "Marc is on his way back."

"Alone?" If he'd met with both men, they would have been very short conversations, considering Seattle was at least a two hour round trip drive.

"Presumably." She glanced toward the door leading out of the library room. "How long do you plan to keep Katrina here?"

"As long as it takes to make sure she's safe."

"How are we going to do that from here?" Carissa asked.

"What do you mean?" Frank trusted Carissa with his life, but right now, she didn't make sense.

"If we're holed up here, how are we supposed to determine if she's truly in danger? What if the driver who appeared to try to hit her was simply not paying attention? He could have easily jumped the curb and chased her up the lawn until he hit her."

"True." And he did swerve at the last minute to avoid a collision with her car. Were they overreacting? Had they misread the situation? "Before we make any plans, we need to learn what Marc knows. Then we'll proceed from there." If he had jumped to the wrong conclusion, he'd at least enjoyed the last few hours with Katrina. He couldn't recall ever baking Christmas cookies with anyone. His mom hadn't liked to share her kitchen and insisted everyone stayed out. But he had sneaked several chunks of dough when she wasn't looking whenever she baked. That was before he understood the potential danger of eating raw dough.

Carissa's expression changed to one of mischief as she narrowed her eyes. "What's up with you and Katrina? Don't tell me nothing either. I'm not blind."

He shrugged. "She's a friend."

"How'd that happen?"

He chuckled. "I suppose I had that coming considering you think all I do is work." He filled her in on how they'd met and how he'd started mowing her lawn. "In short, we clicked, but we're only friends. Nothing more, so get rid of that gleam in your eyes. Not all of us are cut out for relationships."

"We're not?" She actually sounded surprised.

"Of course not. I'm married to my job."

"So am I. But that hasn't stopped me."

Frank raised a brow. "Seems like it might." When he'd heard Marc might leave the team, he'd wanted to crush the man. He could see how hurt Carissa was. He'd do what it took to keep this team together and, hopefully, it'd be enough for his partners because he didn't want things to change.

Katrina glanced at the clock on the oven for the third time in as many minutes. She'd love to know what Frank and his team were saying, but eavesdropping was what got her into this mess, so she'd stay put. She didn't believe for a nanosecond that Jason had anything to do with what was going on. He didn't care enough about her to put out the effort.

Sure, he'd been possessive when they were married, but not because he loved her. He looked at her like a possession and sought to control her. He'd moved on to another woman not too many years after they were divorced.

This mess had to have something to do with work and what she'd overheard. If only she'd gotten a look inside the breakroom to see the men who were talking. Then again, maybe it was a good thing she hadn't. They might have taken her out right in the middle of the bank. She shook away the morbid thought.

The oven timer beeped. She donned a heat-proof glove and pulled out a tray of candy-cane shaped cookies. She'd whip up some frosting soon.

Frank sauntered back into the kitchen. "Mmm. Those sure smell good." He reached toward the hot pan.

She slapped his hand away. "You'll burn yourself. Give them at least a minute to cool."

He huffed a breath. "Fine. I'll have another snickerdoodle."

"I thought you didn't want to go into a sugar coma."

"One more won't hurt." He popped an entire cookie into his mouth.

She chuckled. "I'm glad you like them. Do you know anything new?"

"Marc will be back soon from Seattle. I'll know more when I've been briefed. In the meantime, what do you say we give that oven a break and watch a Christmas movie?"

"I'm not done." She motioned to the dough on the counter.

"You could pop it into the fridge for later."

"I suppose that would be fine." She did as he requested. "But what about the mess? It's not going to clean itself."

He pushed up his sleeves. "I happen to be a pro at washing dishes."

She batted her lashes. "You're my kind of man, Mr. Davis."

He laughed. "And you're a nut." He flipped on the water.

"Nuts are good."

He sobered and caught her gaze. "They certainly are."

Her breath caught, and her heart raced. She lowered her gaze. She had to get them back into safe territory. "Dish soap."

"Huh?"

"It's under the sink. You'll need it for the dishes."

"Uh. Right." He pulled out the soap and squeezed some under the flowing water.

Twenty minutes later, she put the last dish away. "Thanks for the help, Frank. You still want to watch a movie?"

"Of course." He led the way to the couch and reached for the remote right as the front door burst open.

She jumped and whirled around. "Oh, it's only you. You about gave me a heart attack."

"Sorry," Marc said. "Frank, do you want to meet me in the library?"

Frank nodded. "Be back soon. Go ahead and pick out something." He gently squeezed her shoulder and left the room.

Frank closed the door behind him.

She'd give almost anything to be a fly on the wall in that room. Sure the team seemed to keep her up to date about what was going on, but what if they were afraid she couldn't handle something? She needed to know anything and everything that pertained to her safety.

She might regret this, but she couldn't help herself. She tiptoed to the closed door where Frank and his team were meeting. She turned her head with her ear to the door and strained to listen.

"The FBI didn't find anything to cause concern regarding Katrina," Marc said.

"Good," Carissa said. "So he thinks we can trust what she says."

"I can't believe you doubted." Frank sounded annoyed. "I thought you trusted my judgment."

"We do," Carissa said. "Your heart is another matter."

Katrina's breath caught in her throat. She pressed her ear to the door anxious for Frank's response.

The deep rumble of his voice sounded, but his words were indistinguishable. The door flew open.

Katrina gasped and fell forward into his arms. She looked up at him. "Uh…hi." Her face heated as she scrambled out of his gentle hold.

Frank frowned. "Hi, yourself. Could you please come in? Though I suspect you already heard everything."

Katrina's heart raced. "Not really." She stepped into the room. "What's going on?"

"The FBI is interested in what you heard." Marc handed her an envelope. "That's a letter explaining what they want you to do."

"Have you read it?" She took the envelope and stared at it. Fear shot through her. What could they possibly want from her?

"I haven't, but I was briefed on the contents."

She nodded, swallowed the lump in her throat, and then pulled out a folded piece of paper. She scanned the letter. "They want me to return to work on Monday. I'm allowed to talk about the explosion at my house, but beyond that, I'm supposed to go on as normal." She looked up and focused on Frank. "Please forgive my hesitation, but this sounds like a dangerous idea. What if I'm right and someone at the bank wants to harm me?"

Frank's eyes held sympathy. "I've worked with this agent. I don't think he would ask this of you without a solid plan in place."

Marc cleared his throat. "What the letter doesn't say is that an undercover agent will be subbing for one of the security guards this week. You'll be perfectly safe while you're at work."

She nodded. "Okay. That does make me feel a little better. Where will the three of you be?"

They all exchanged a look. Frank cleared his throat. "We've been ordered by the FBI to stand down. But that won't stop us from looking into who could be behind this. We'll just need to be more discreet. When you're off work, I'll be there to drive you home."

"Where exactly is home?"

"This could be home for the week. I realize the commute will be a pain, but it's only for a week."

"I don't want to put you out like that."

"It's not an imposition. It's a nice change of scenery. Much better than the view I have from my place."

He had a point. The property here was beautiful with the surrounding trees, and the view from his place contained her wreck of a house. She included Marc and Carissa in her gaze. "What about the two of you? I know you had plans for this week."

"We did," Carissa said. "But I'm with Frank on this. It's a nice change in scenery here. We could even decorate it for Christmas. I noticed a few boxes in the garage marked Christmas."

A tremble of excitement shot through Katrina. It had been years since she'd experienced a Christmas like what Carissa was suggesting. Was it wishful thinking though? Could they really have a festive atmosphere with what was going on?

"What do you say, Katrina?" Marc asked.

Peace unlike anything she'd felt in days washed over her. She grinned. "I'm in. I think I might be losing my mind, but I'm kind of excited. This could be fun."

Frank dipped his chin. "She's a thrill junkie. I had no idea."

They all laughed.

8

Monday morning Katrina walked through the front doors of the bank. Hmm… a new security. He must be the FBI agent. Should she talk to him? She would if it were anyone else. "Good morning."

He nodded.

It seemed that was as good as it would get. This man was intense. Good. Whatever it took to keep everyone safe was fine with her. Shouldn't there be a second guard like usual? She glanced around for John or Drake but didn't spot either man. Hopefully, one of them was in the bathroom. She climbed the stairs to the lockers outside the breakroom to deposit her personal items.

Rick stepped out of his office and looked down his long nose at her.

"Good morning." She didn't bother waiting for a reply. This is how it went every morning. She had half a mind to wish him a Merry Christmas. Though seeing the annoyance on his face for not using the preferred phrase *happy holidays* and the impending lecture silenced the rebellious thought.

She unlocked the cabinet and stuffed her belongings inside.

"I didn't expect to see you. I read a news story that you were missing and that your house blew up."

She turned and faced him. "As you can see, I'm not missing. The reporter only had half the story correct. My home had a gas leak, and the garage was destroyed along with a small portion of my home. The rest has a great deal of damage, but what can't be fixed, can be rebuilt."

He frowned. "Wow. That's so crazy. I'm glad you're okay."

"Thanks." She hadn't expected anything nice to come from his lips. Maybe the Christmas spirit was affecting him. "Excuse me. I need to get to work." She strode past him, wondering at his frown. Did he wish she'd died in the explosion? No. That couldn't be why he'd looked unhappy. He probably frowned because of what had happened. She'd assumed if anyone here at the bank was behind the explosion, it was the men she'd overheard in the breakroom. Her boss was many things, but an attempted murderer hadn't crossed her mind— unless he'd been in the breakroom before surprising her. She shook the thought away, refusing to dwell on the idea.

She strode past a baby grand piano that had been brought in last week as part of a community outreach with the hope of bringing in new customers. Local students from piano studios would be performing every day during the noon hour. Whoever thought that was a good idea hadn't considered the inherent dangers of a crowded bank. Sure, their lobby was generous in size, but if too many friends and family accompanied those students it could get uncomfortable.

John crossed the lobby, heading toward Katrina. "Looks like it'll be a busy day." He nodded to a stand that held the performance schedule.

"I love Christmas music. I only hope they play well."

John chuckled. "Me too. Guess I'd better move to my post." He turned and headed to a lesser-used door that gave him a good view of the entire lobby.

The morning moved right along. She filled in where needed and met with a few clients who had appointments. Around eleven forty-five a commotion at the entrance drew her attention. Young people of all ages crowded near the entrance.

Mr. FBI looked uncertain. Clearly, someone hadn't informed him about this week's entertainment. She checked the performance schedule then stood and strolled over to the gathering crowd. "Are all of you here with Kitts Studio?"

Several heads bobbed.

"Welcome. Please move this direction so we can keep a clear path to the entrance." She guided them to a roped off area not far from the piano. At least her boss had thought to create a designated space for spectators.

She couldn't fathom why Rick had scheduled this during one of their busiest times of day. It didn't make sense to her, but maybe he thought since it was the lunch hour it would be easier for parents to attend. He was always on the prowl for more customers. She glanced toward the stairs wondering when Rick would make an appearance. From what she'd understood, he planned to greet their "guests" and pitch the bank's services to the parents.

A little girl tugged at the hem of Katrina's red sweater. "Is there a potty here?"

She kept the key to the restroom on her wrist bracelet. "Yes. Right this way." She unlocked the restroom and then headed back to her desk.

A moment later, Rick marched down the stairs and over to the crowd of about twenty adults and their kids. "Welcome to B.K.N Bank. We are proud to be able to host events for the community. As many of you might know, B.K.N. donated…"

Katrina tuned out the man's speech. She had better things to do with her time. She logged back onto her computer and got busy. A short while later, an ambitious version of "Jingle Bell Rock" interrupted her thoughts. As much as she liked the lively tune, a peaceful song like "Silent Night" would have been much more conducive to working.

Ten minutes into the performances, a man wearing a tan trench coat strolled into the bank. There was something about him that made her uneasy. She looked at the FBI agent who watched the man walk to the line for the tellers.

What should she do? Her heart rate kicked up a notch. She looked toward John at the other door. He didn't seem concerned by the man, but his focus had been on the musicians.

For the umpteenth time, she wished she'd not overheard that conversation. Her mind was probably playing tricks on her. FBI agent or not, unease consumed her. She wouldn't feel settled until the students were safely out of the bank and the crowded lobby more resembled a normal Monday afternoon.

"How's it going?"

Katrina jumped and whipped her head in the direction of the familiar voice. "Frank? What are you doing here?"

"Thought we could grab lunch." He glanced toward the piano and the group of onlookers. "This is a happening place."

"Right? I'd love to get lunch, but I can't until one."

"No problem. I'll wait." He motioned to the small sitting area where customers waited to talk to loan officers. "Is over there okay?"

She glanced to the second level. Not that it mattered if her boss was looking over the balcony since he had real-time surveillance cameras everywhere with access in his office. Come to think of it, a person would be foolish to rob this place, all things considered.

"Katrina?" Frank asked.

"Oh, yes. Sorry. Over there is fine. Are you sure you want to wait? I don't want to keep you from something." She lowered her voice. "I thought the FBI said to back off. You aren't supposed to be here."

"I'm on vacation, remember? My time is my own to do with as I please, and this place is quite the find. I'm here to take my beautiful neighbor and friend to lunch. They can't fault me for that."

He'd called her beautiful. That wasn't a term she'd often been attached to. What was he up to? She shook away her suspicious thought. Frank wouldn't say something he didn't mean, and like they said, beauty is in the eyes of the beholder.

Frank looked around the lobby. "Carissa would love it in here with the music and festive decorations."

She had noticed Christmas decorations were important to the woman—that and good coffee. They'd spent the better part of Sunday decking out the house in Warm Beach for Christmas. Marc and Frank had set up a tree, and she and Carissa had wrapped it in more lights than she thought safe, but the younger woman had insisted there was no such thing as too many lights.

Katrina grinned. "I think you're right about Carissa. But since I'm *not* on vacation, I'd better get back to work." She glanced toward the man in the trench coat who stood in line. He still gave her the creeps, but with Frank here, she wasn't so worried. It was funny how the mere presence of her neighbor made her less afraid.

A few minutes later, the man who'd raised the hair on her neck left before he got to the teller window. Odd but she didn't care, so long as he was gone. She breathed easy for the first time in five minutes. She definitely needed to get a grip if the mere presence of a man in a trench coat sent her imagination into overdrive. One o'clock finally came, and the musical interlude ended. She stood and mouthed to Frank that she'd be right back.

She trotted up the stairs and quickly retrieved her purse and jacket.

Rick stood in his doorway. "Who's the man in the waiting area?"

"My neighbor. We're getting lunch. He forgot I take a late one."

Rick nodded but didn't say a word. He turned and went back to his desk, leaving the door open.

She trotted down the stairs and met Frank beside the door to the bank. "Where would you like to go?"

"Somewhere that's quick, tasty, and serves a hot meal."

"I know the place." She smiled at the FBI guy as they headed out and then made a right and headed for her favorite lunchtime eatery. Wind whipped her hair into her face. She pulled her hood over her head, noting Frank's furrowed brows and attention to their surroundings. She slowed her pace. Something was up. "Why did you really stop by the bank?"

"What gave me away? I thought you bought my

lunch excuse. Though I really am hungry for a hot meal."

"You had me going, but I noticed you're in protection mode. What's going on?"

"There was a credible tip that something was going down at the bank this morning."

Her stomach lurched. "Nothing happened."

"I noticed."

She stopped outside her usual lunch haunt.

"This it?" Frank asked.

She nodded.

He pulled open the door. "After you."

They each ordered a bowl of soup with a side of sourdough bread.

Frank led her to an out-of-the-way table. "We should be able to talk privately here."

She sat beside him, facing the door with the wall to her back. It seemed like a good spot since no one would be able to sneak up on them from behind. "So tell me more. Do you think someone tipped off the bad guys?"

He reached for his spoon and shrugged. "Hard to know for sure. I'm glad nothing happened though, especially with all those kids there."

She bit down on her bottom lip.

Frank's hand, which held his spoon, stopped midway to his mouth. "Uh-oh. What don't I know?" He set his spoon in the bowl.

"A man walked in shortly before you. He made me feel uneasy. As in the hairs on my neck stood up. Even the security guard seemed interested as if he thought the man was up to something. Then the man left without incident."

"Hmm." He picked up his utensil again and shoveled a spoonful of creamy potato soup into his mouth.

"What does hmm mean?" She followed his example and got busy eating the minestrone she'd ordered.

"It's curious, that's all. The hair on my neck only stands up in a true emergency. I wonder…"

"What?" Her voice rose and a few people looked their direction. "Sorry. What do you wonder?"

"You're talking about the man in the tan trench coat, right?"

Her jaw dropped. "How did you know?"

"I had a feeling about him too. I was at the corner of the block when I saw him walk in. Something was off with him."

"Yet nothing happened. Do you think he thought you were a cop?"

"No clue, but considering the crowd in there, it would've been the perfect time to rob the bank. Or maybe the crowd is what dissuaded him. Did you recognize him?"

"No. I feel like whoever I overheard talking had to work for the bank or else why would they be in the breakroom?"

"I noticed the bank is large, but I didn't see a lot of people working out in the open."

She nodded. "There are offices in back for our loan processors and others that don't work directly with the public."

"Aren't you a loan processor?"

"Not really. I'm a loan officer as well as help new customers open accounts." She didn't care to go into her job description. "Is it safe for me to go back to work today?"

"I think so, but if you'd like for me to hang out, I can." His relaxed demeanor suggested he meant the offer.

"Thanks, but I don't think my boss would like it. He asked about you."

Frank's brows rose. "Is that normal?"

"Beats me. I've never had anyone besides customers waiting for me." She glanced at her watch. "We need to eat faster. I can't be late."

"It's only a five-minute walk. We'll be fine."

"Just the same." She was hungry and couldn't eat and talk politely.

They focused on their food for the next several minutes.

"Carissa is in the city today. I might have her pop into the bank a bit later. Scope out the place. She has a knack for noticing things others miss."

"If she could pretend to be a customer that would be helpful. Rick didn't get angry when I told him you were my neighbor and we were going to lunch, but I don't want to push my luck."

"Understood. I'd like to meet him."

"I suppose I could introduce you if you want to walk back to work with me."

"I'd appreciate that." Frank mopped up the remainder of his soup with the slice of bread. "That was great. Do you come here often?"

She patted her stomach. "Too often. I know I shouldn't eat out every day, but I can't get myself to stay at the bank during lunch. You ready to go?"

"Don't you get a full hour?"

She nodded. "But I like to return early." A commotion outside drew her attention. "I wonder what's going on."

Frank stood. "How about you sit tight. I'll check it out."

She nodded. Ordinarily, she'd insist on looking for herself, but life had been too nuts the past few days. She knew Frank only had her safety in mind with his request.

A couple minutes later, he strode back inside. "You won't believe this." He sat down beside her. "The bank was just robbed."

Her stomach lurched. She bolted to standing. "I need to get over there."

He reached for her hand and tugged gently. "What you need to do is sit tight for a few minutes. Let the police get on-site and allow things to settle down a bit."

She checked the time. "I'm supposed to start working in fifteen minutes."

"You have time. Give it five minutes."

She sighed. "I'm trying to cooperate and be agreeable, but you, sir, are making it difficult."

He chuckled. "Sorry."

Frank had no intention of allowing Katrina to walk to the bank without him, especially with how pale she'd turned when he'd told her about the bank robbery. While he was outside, he'd sent a text to Dillon to see if he knew anything. He didn't. Then he'd called Marc to let him know what went down and see if he'd talk with Kyle. Hopefully, the special agent would let them know what the FBI knew, but with his track record, it wasn't likely.

"Can we leave now?" Katrina pleaded with him. "Please."

"Yes. We've probably waited long enough." He doubted the authorities would allow her inside the bank, but there was no harm in trying. He stood and grasped her hand. He didn't want to lose her in the commotion outside. He pulled open the door then headed out. A cold wind smacked him in the face. If it got much colder, they might have a white Christmas.

"Look at all those police cars." Awe filled Katrina's voice. "Maybe I should call Rick."

"You could, or you could wait a few minutes and talk to him in person." If she called her boss, it reduced the chance of him meeting the man face to face, something he'd wanted to do since Katrina brought him up a few days ago. He wanted to get a read on the man. See if he could be trusted.

"I'm not sure they'll let us past that barricade."

He shrugged. "We'll see." They pushed through the gathering crowd of onlookers until they reached the barricade. He released her hand and checked out the situation. An officer he knew walked toward them. "Hi, Barry. This is Katrina. She works at the bank. We were having a late lunch. Is there any way she could get inside?"

Barry frowned. "I'm afraid not. It's a crime scene. If you need something, one of the officers could bring it to you."

She shook her head. "No. I have my belongings, but I'm concerned about getting in trouble with my boss. I'm on the clock."

"Your boss is the bank manager?"

"Yes."

"Hold tight. Be right back."

Katrina looked at Frank. "This is so surreal."

"It's weird all right. But not entirely unexpected."

Katrina spoke close to his ear. "Did Rick know about the tip?"

"I don't know." That was a very good question. If he knew, would he have allowed the students to perform anyway? The man in question walked outside with Officer Barry and headed their direction.

He stopped on the other side of the barricade. Barry stood beside him.

"Is everyone okay?" Katrina asked.

"Mostly." Rick's pallor spoke volumes to his headspace. "The bank will be closed until the police are finished with their investigation and I can get a crew in there to clean. You may go home. I'll see you tomorrow, assuming they're finished. I'll be sending an e-mail this evening to everyone so watch for it."

"Okay. Was the robber caught?"

Rick looked toward the officer. "The new security officer took Gary from the loan department down. He was in disguise but after..." He shook his head. "I can't believe someone who worked here would do that."

"As in shot him?" Katrina asked. "Is everyone else okay?"

Rick nodded. "But it's not pretty in there. I'm trying to be positive, though I'm not sure we'll be able to open tomorrow even if the crime scene has been cleared. It's going to take a special cleaning crew to—"

"We understand." Frank didn't want the visual in Katrina's mind. She'd been through enough with her home and then almost getting run down. "I'm Frank, a friend of Katrina's." He held out his hand.

Rick grasped it firmly then released his hand. "It's nice to meet you, though I wish it was under different circumstance. Excuse me. I should get back inside. I'll be in touch, Katrina. By the way, where are you staying?"

"In—" Katrina said.

"With me." Frank narrowed his eyes. There was no way her boss needed that information.

Rick looked from him to Katrina with insinuation on his face.

"Her house was destroyed last week. I'm sure you heard."

"Right. You're quite the *friendly* neighbor."

Frank puffed out his chest. "I don't care for what you're insinuating."

Rick raised his hands palms out. "Sorry. No harm meant. It's been a day."

"That it has." Frank waited for the man to walk back inside and then turned to Katrina. "You ready to go?"

Fire lit her eyes. "I'm sorry about Rick."

"Don't be. He was right; it's been a day."

"It sure has. Let's get out of here."

He liked the sound of that. The sooner he got her away from this crowd the better. "Do you mind if we swing by Marc's place before heading back." Marc had called before everything went nuts with a special request that both floored him and excited him at the same time. They were close as brothers once upon a time, but since they'd become business partners, they'd been too busy for a good heart-to-heart.

"Not at all. What's up?"

"He has a little surprise planned. He asked me to pick up a very special order for him at his local grocery store and then to head over."

"Sounds intriguing?" Katrina raised a brow.

"Oh, it is. I have a feeling we'll be walking in on a very happy couple when we arrive." If he was wrong though, things were going to become mighty awkward at Protection Inc.

9

Marc wiped his palms down the side of his jeans. Carissa looked at him and frowned. "Are you feeling okay?" He sure seemed nervous. If she didn't know better, she'd think he was about to propose.

"Uh, yeah. There's something I wanted to ask you." He took a deep breath and, facing Carissa, dropped to one knee in the middle of his living room.

Tingles shot through her. Was he really going to propose, or was this something else?

Marc cleared his throat. "This isn't the way I had planned, but I can't wait another minute."

She gasped. "Are you doing what I think you're doing?"

He reached out a hand and wrapped his around hers. "I love you, Carissa, and I want to spend the rest of my life with you. Will you marry me?"

"I thought you were ready to give up on us because of our schedules. I'm so confused."

Marc's face turned a light pink. "I've had a lot of

time to think since Saturday. If we're married, we'll see each other all the time." He grinned. "Plus, with the new game plan for weekends..."

Carissa grinned. "Ah, now I understand. I like the way you're thinking." She took his hand and pulled him up. "Of course I'll marry you."

Marc rested one hand on her cheek and the other on her waist. "I thought we could pick out rings together."

"Really? Or is it more like you hadn't planned to propose and didn't have a ring?"

"Oh no, I was going to propose this week. Christmas Eve to be exact, but we've never talked rings, and I want you to have one you'll like."

She ran her hands up his chest then around his neck. "I had no idea how considerate and thoughtful you could be. There's this great little jewelry shop in Lincoln City where we can go while we're visiting my parents." Who was she kidding? The chances they'd actually get to Oregon for Christmas were slim to none.

"That sounds good to me, but you know we might not make it to your parents', right?" He spoke softly, his breath tickling her cheek.

"You talk too much." She brushed her lips to his.

A firm knock split the air.

Carissa groaned. "Someone has very bad timing."

"Or very good." Marc pecked her lips then turned and strode to the door. "Frank, good to see you. You too, Katrina. Come in. Did you pick up that order?"

"I did, but it's in the car. After I saw what it was, I thought I should wait and check with you first."

Carissa couldn't help hearing their entire conversation in the small apartment even though they weren't in the same room. What order was Marc talking about?

"Ye of little faith," Marc said.

Carissa popped around the corner as Marc clapped Frank on the shoulder and nudged him toward the door.

Frank chuckled. "Be right back."

Katrina strolled toward Carissa. "I hear congratulations are in order."

Carissa nodded. She must be glowing with happiness.

Katrina reached for her left hand and frowned. "Where's your ring?"

"At the jewelry store. We'll pick out rings together."

"How romantic."

A minute later, Frank and Marc walked into the living room. Marc held a dozen red roses with a Mylar balloon in the shape of a diamond ring attached to a bottle of sparkling cider.

Carissa chuckled. "My ring!" She teased. "It's bigger than I ever imagined."

Marc's eyes smoldered with love. He handed her the roses. "For you."

Her face warmed. "Thanks."

Frank cleared his throat. "There's a small engagement cake too."

Carissa looked between the two men who meant so much to her. "Really?"

Marc grinned.

"What if I'd said no?"

"Then Katrina and I would have devoured it on our way back to Warm Beach." Frank held the cake. "Want to have it now or later?"

"Later," Marc and Carissa said at the same time.

Katrina laughed. "You two are perfect for one another."

Regardless of everything, Carissa couldn't have asked for a better proposal and people to celebrate with. "What do you say we head out now before traffic gets too bad?"

"Sounds perfect." Frank handed Marc the cake. "We'll meet you there." He rested his hand on Katrina's back as they left Marc's apartment.

Deep joy bubbled up in Carissa. She laughed and happy-danced in place.

Marc's jaw dropped. "Are you okay?"

"Yes. This is me very happy."

"Good to know. What do you say we get out of here and finish celebrating at the house?"

An hour later, they walked into Peter's house. A fire crackled in the fireplace, and the scent of Mexican food filled the air.

"What smells so good?" Marc asked.

"Tamales. Katrina is a wiz in the kitchen," Frank said with a gleam in his eyes.

Carissa bit back a smile. The love bug had bitten her longtime friend and business partner. Did he realize it yet?

Katrina enjoyed cooking, but she liked making her heroes happy even more. These people had sacrificed a lot to make sure she stayed safe. She knew it couldn't go on forever, but she'd appreciate it while it lasted.

By her best guess, she had until New Years at the latest. Then she would be on her own again and in desperate need of a place to live. Tomorrow, she'd find out from her insurance when she could get started with repairs to her home. She should have already reached out to some contractors, but she'd been surprisingly busy.

Frank leaned over her shoulder as she stirred the spicy red sauce she'd made to serve with the tamales. He breathed in deeply. "That seriously smells amazing. How much longer 'til we eat?"

"As soon as the rice is finished. I can't believe you're so hungry. We had a late lunch, and it hasn't been that long."

"Lady, I can eat any time." He stepped back and patted his stomach.

And what a fine stomach it was. She laughed. It felt good, but her mood quickly shifted to worry.

"What's the matter?" Frank leaned against the counter beside the stove.

"Please don't think I'm ungrateful, but I'm concerned about what's going to happen to me after you and your team's vacation ends. Specifically, where I'm going to live."

He frowned. "We'll figure it out."

"It's not your job to figure out my life. But I do appreciate that you're willing to help." She laid the whisk on the spoon rest. "When do you think we'll know if I'm truly in danger?"

"I suppose the best way to find that out is to go out in public more. See if we're followed."

"Isn't that risky? What if we're followed back here?" She shook her head. "I wouldn't want Peter's home destroyed like mine was."

Frank blew out a slow breath. "Nor would I. Honestly, I don't know how to proceed. I'm flying by the seat of my pants."

She studied him a moment. He seemed relaxed. "That's normal?"

"More than I'd like. We've done everything we can for now. I realize it's frustrating not knowing what's going to happen next, but please know we are all on your side, and we'll do everything in our power to keep you safe."

She ran her hands up and down her bare arms. "I hate not being in control of my own life or at least feeling like I'm in control." She laughed drily. "I suppose control is an illusion."

"What do you mean?" Frank asked.

"Even when I feel like I'm in control, I'm not. It only takes the act of one person to throw my world out of balance."

"Interesting. That seems to be a theme of late. But I guess I understand. It kind of reminds me of my relationship with the Lord. I want to take charge and be in control all the time. I have to constantly remind myself to slow down and listen for His plan."

"I forgot you're a Christian."

"What about you? Are you one?"

"I'm not a religious person, but I believe in God."

Frank pulled a glass from the cupboard and filled it with water from the faucet. "Funny thing about religion. I don't think Christianity and religion are the same."

"What do you mean?" She pulled the rice off the burner then reached for a serving bowl.

"To me, religion is formal—a rules and regulation kind of thing. Whereas Christianity should be relationship driven."

"You mean a relationship with God?"

"Yes and His Son, Jesus."

"Interesting. I've honestly never given it a lot of thought."

"Maybe you should. I treasure the peace and hope I have with Him." He pulled open the oven door. "The tamales look done to me."

She looked inside. "Yep." She handed him two hot pads and then finished with the rice and sauce and took it to the table.

"Dinner," Frank hollered.

Marc and Carissa ambled in from the library.

"Mmm," Carissa said. "If you ever decide to leave the banking business, you could have a career in the kitchen."

Katrina smiled. "Thanks." She would seriously miss these people when life went back to normal. Though she wouldn't miss the fear that someone could be trying to kill her.

10

Carissa and Marc snuggled on the couch after dinner. Katrina had retreated to the bedroom and Frank to the library.

"I've been thinking about Katrina's living situation." Marc ran his thumb up and down Carissa's shoulder where his hand rested.

"And?"

"I'd like to let her sublet my apartment, assuming she's interested."

Carissa pulled out of his arms and faced him. "Where would you live?"

"With you. We can get married before the first of the year, and I can move into your place."

That would be a lightning-fast engagement. She was still getting used to the idea of being engaged. After all, it had only been a few hours, and now he wanted a wedding in less than two weeks.

Marc reached for her hands. "Say something."

"It's a lot to process. You haven't even met my parents. I'd want them to be at our ceremony."

"We could elope." A hopeful look filled his eyes. "My family is complicated, and it'd be a lot easier for me."

"I don't know." Not that she was one of those women who'd been planning the wedding of her dreams since she was a girl, but she did have some expectations. A big one was sharing the event with those she cared most about. "I need to talk with my mom." She stood.

"Where are you going?"

Good question. She wanted privacy. "I guess I'll go outside." She'd need a hat and gloves. Fortunately, both were beside the door. She slipped into her winter wear, flipped on the porch light, and then went outside. At least it was above freezing.

She slipped her earbuds into her ears and placed the call. Her mom's phone rang for the third time.

"This is a surprise," her mom said. "When will you and Marc get here?"

Carissa fought to control her emotions. She'd never felt so torn, but she was where she needed to be right now. "Something came up, and I'm not sure we'll make it at all. Frank's neighbor needs our help."

"Oh."

Carissa's throat thickened. "Here's the thing. Marc asked me to marry him."

Mom gasped. "I didn't realize you were so serious, but I suppose I should have since he had planned to come here for Christmas. Congratulations."

"Thanks. I have a feeling he probably wanted to

talk to you and Dad this week, but things are kind of nuts here, and our client needs a place to live for several months since her home exploded."

"Exploded?" Mom's voice rose in pitch.

"Yes. It's being called a freak accident. A gas leak in the garage."

"You don't agree?"

"I'm not convinced." A four-legged creature scuttled across the driveway. She sure hoped that wasn't a skunk. At least the door was right behind her.

"Why?"

She tried to ignore the possibility of nocturnal creatures venturing too close to the house and focused on her conversation. "For starters, what could have set it off? No one was in there to ignite an explosion. It doesn't add up. I believe there was an explosive device in her garage that went off and someone is covering it up."

Mom gasped. "Oh, Carissa. Please be careful."

"I'm always careful, but now that you know what's going on here, I need to know what to do." She loved her mom. Though they weren't as close as they once were, she still could count on Mom for sound wisdom. "Marc wants to get married before New Year's. I don't know what to do."

Mom chuckled softly. "You do get yourself into some crazy situations. I would think you'd want a traditional wedding."

"I did, but if we get married right away, that would

free up his apartment for Frank's neighbor until her home is repaired."

"Ah. Now I understand. Two things you should keep in mind. There are other places she can live, and you aren't her savior—her protector, yes, but definitely not her savior. I suggest you trust your heart. Listen to what it's saying."

"What if I can't hear it?" She couldn't wrap her mind around the fact she was engaged and might be married in less than two weeks. Did she really want that? Her knee-jerk response was no.

"I suggest you and Marc talk. Whatever you decide, you have our blessing, but you better not get married without us. I don't care if it's a civil service in the courthouse. I want to be there."

She grinned. "Okay. I'll keep you updated."

"I love you, and I have confidence you'll make the right decision."

"Thanks." Carissa ended the call. Her mom's belief in her decision making exceeded her own. *What do I do, Lord?*

She leaned against the house and closed her eyes. She wanted to marry Marc, but she didn't want to rush a wedding. Didn't want to marry quickly out of convenience. She wanted the dream. Wanted a wedding dress, a cake, and flowers. She wasn't a girly girl, but those things mattered to her.

The door opened slowly. Marc stood there with his hands in his pockets. "Want to take a walk?"

She nodded. "But I want my Glock." She brushed past him and quickly armed herself. Who knew what was out there in the dark.

Once on the front porch, he turned to her and grasped her hands in his. "I'm sorry."

"For what?"

"Rushing you to get married. We can wait however long it takes to plan the wedding you want. Maybe Peter will rent this place to her for a couple of months."

"That's actually a good idea. Apology accepted." He'd made her decision so much easier. "Whatever we do, my parents want to be there."

"I understand. If we have a wedding, my family will probably show up too."

Which she knew he wanted to avoid. There had to be a compromise that would make them both happy. "I thought you wanted to walk."

He grinned and strolled beside her. They ambled toward the trees. "What else did your mom say? Is she upset about Christmas?"

"Hmm. We didn't talk much about it, but if there's any way we can get down there, I want to. It won't feel like Christmas unless I'm at my parents' place."

"I don't know. They're predicting a white Christmas here. It's not likely where they live."

"You're assuming I want snow."

"You don't?"

Snow was fine, but she'd rather be home than in her apartment. "It's not my favorite. It makes getting around a challenge."

"What would make you happy this Christmas?" Marc stopped walking and pulled her close. His warm body pressed against hers.

"Being home with a cozy fire burning in the fireplace, soft music playing in the background, and my dad passing out the gifts." She hadn't realized it until seconds ago, but she missed her family's traditional Christmas and more than anything wanted to go home to her parents' place.

"I hope you get your wish."

She sighed. "It's not likely this year. I'm not comfortable with either of us leaving Frank and Katrina here alone. What if something were to happen?"

"Like what?"

"Like whoever is after her finds her while we're gone."

"Okay. You make a valid point. I'll pray we wrap this up and are able to get to Oregon by Christmas."

"Thank you." She pulled her head back slightly and pressed her lips to his.

He deepened the kiss.

A shot rang out.

They lurched apart and dove to the ground then crawled toward the nearest tree.

Frank's head jerked at the sound of gunfire. He flicked off the lights and raced to Katrina's room.

She stood in the doorway. "Did you hear a gunshot?"

"Yes. Are you okay?"

"I'm fine. It was probably a hunter. Don't you think?" Her voice wobbled slightly. Clearly she was in denial.

"Wrong caliber." Of all times for Marc and Carissa to be outside. He called 9-1-1 and reported shots fired. Then pressed Carissa's number rather than Marc's since she always kept her phone on vibrate. If they were under fire, the phone vibrations shouldn't give their location away.

She answered on the first ring. "Frank, you okay in there?"

"Yes. I was going to ask you the same."

"So far. We don't know which direction the shot came from," she whispered.

"Understood. Can you get to the house?"

"Unknown."

His gut churned. "Are you at least armed?"

"Affirmative."

"Good. Cover us. We'll be coming out the front door. I want to get Katrina out of here." Thankfully, his SUV was parked near the door so the risk would be minimal.

"Give us a minute to get into position. I'll text when we're ready."

"Got it." He pocketed his phone. "Grab what you can't live without, Katrina. We're making a run for it."

She ran to the bedroom and returned with a large purse-like bag. She quickly grabbed a bag of cookies from the freezer and stuffed it into the bag.

He shook his head. "Seriously? That's absolutely necessary?"

"What? I worked hard to make these. I'm not going to let someone with a gun keep me from enjoying my favorite Christmas tradition."

He blew out a breath. "I can't argue with that reasoning." He'd send someone back for the rest of their belongings later. Right now, his primary concern was getting Katrina to safety.

Another shot shattered a window.

"Guess there's no doubt of a threat now." He gritted his teeth. "Time to go." His phone chimed indicating a text. He glanced at it. They were ready. He rushed Katrina to the front door and slowly opened it. Carissa and Marc stood at the ready on each side of the door. They'd cover Katrina with their own bodies.

Marc nodded, indicating they were ready.

"Stay crouched and stay between us. Move as quickly as you can. When we get to my SUV climb into the backseat and get on the floor. Stay low no matter what."

"Okay."

"Go." They rushed out.

Another shot rang out. Pain stabbed Frank's shoulder. He sucked in a sharp breath. "Move faster." He dove onto the passenger seat.

Carissa followed Katrina into the back and Marc got behind the wheel.

"Keys," Marc said.

Frank palmed them to him.

Marc did a double take. "You were hit."

"I'm aware. Now get us out of here."

Marc started the vehicle and floored the gas. Gravel flew and they fishtailed then shot forward. "Sorry." Marc gripped the steering wheel with two hands and drove. "Where to?"

Frank hesitated. He'd thought the bullet grazed him, but now he wasn't certain. "Head toward Seattle." He grabbed a handful of napkins from the glove box and pressed them to his shoulder. "There are closer hospitals, but I'd prefer to be in Seattle." He called Dillon and filled him in on their situation. "What do you suggest?"

"Are you losing a lot of blood?"

Frank looked down at his shoulder. "A fair amount. I'm thinking University Medical Center."

"I'll meet you there. If anything changes, let me know. I'll alert the hospital to expect you."

"Will do. And thanks."

"I heard," Marc said. "We're headed to the university hospital."

"Are we being followed?" Carissa asked.

"Not that I can tell," Marc said. "Pray no critters run out in front of us."

Frank understood the request. They were speeding

on a country road to get to I-5. It appeared someone had followed them back to the house from Seattle. How had they missed seeing a tail? He blew out a breath.

"You doing okay?" Marc asked. "There are closer hospitals."

"I'm okay. Just frustrated with this turn of events."

"I don't know how they found us. I was careful. I know no one followed me back to the house."

"Same," Frank said. If neither of them had been followed, they'd been tracked another way. Cell phone perhaps? Or a tracker on one of their vehicles? He'd been parked in Seattle for a few hours today. Anyone could have put a tracker under his bumper. He should have checked. "Pull over."

"No way. What if they're trying to catch up?"

"If I'm right, it won't matter how fast we go. Pull over."

Marc slowed and pulled off to the side at the next driveway. "Now what?"

"Get out and look for a tracking device under my rig."

Marc grabbed his phone and engaged the flashlight app. "You really think that's how we were found?"

"I do."

Marc got out and a couple minutes later sat behind the wheel. He held out the palm of his hand.

"You found it."

"What do I do with it?"

Frank reached for it. "We disengage it." He turned off the device. "Now let's move."

Marc put the SUV in gear and pulled out onto the road.

"I think it's safe for you to sit on the seat now, Katrina," Carissa said. "Be sure to buckle in. Marc has a lead foot."

Katrina settled onto the seat. The sound of metal hitting plastic over and over sounded. "I can't buckle it." Frustration and despair laced her voice.

"Let me." Carissa reached across the seat and clicked the buckle.

Marc took the onramp to the freeway.

Frank leaned back and closed his eyes. He'd caused this. They were a team, but it was his fault they were in this situation. He had thought taking Katrina to an out of the way location would keep her safe. He'd been wrong.

"Frank," Katrina's voice shook. "Are you sure you want to go all the way to Seattle. What if you lose too much blood?"

Frank flicked on the overhead light and looked at his shoulder and his stomach roiled. "I'm okay. No lightheadedness yet."

"Take it from me," Carissa said. "I was in a similar situation not all that long ago, and I got lightheaded from loss of blood. I think you're fine to wait until we get to Seattle unless something changes."

"Thanks, Dr. Jones." Maybe if he kept things light, Katrina wouldn't freak out about his gunshot wound. He was doing that enough for all of them. His dominant arm had been winged—not good.

"You're a doctor too?" Katrina asked.

"No. That was Frank trying to be funny."

"Guess I failed. It's not my day."

Marc laughed drily. "I'd say it's not any of our days. On the bright side, I have an idea for where Katrina can stay until her home is fixed. Katrina can sublet my place, and I can bunk at yours, Frank."

"I don't recall anyone asking me if I wanted to sublet your place." Annoyance filled Katrina's voice.

"You don't?" they all asked in unison.

"What I don't want is to be dictated to. Right now my thoughts are all jumbled."

Frank winced as he glanced over his shoulder to look at Katrina. "Guess we were so focused on protecting you, we forgot to ask what you wanted. When you can think straight, please figure out where you'd like to live while your home is being put back together."

"Okay, but one problem at a time," she said. "Right now, we need to focus on getting you to the hospital. After that, we can talk to the authorities. Needless to say, I'm *not* going back to work at the bank even if it does open tomorrow. That place is trouble, and I want nothing more to do with it. I'll e-mail my resignation effective immediately."

"Are you sure?" Carissa asked. "You shouldn't make any big decisions while under duress. Maybe think on it for a couple of days. I'm sure your boss would understand if you need some time off after what went down at the bank today."

"Yeah. I suppose you're right. Thank you for keeping me from doing something rash. But there's one thing that I really don't understand."

"What's that?" Carissa asked.

"Who wants me dead? The bank robber was killed. His partner is in the wind. I can't identify either of them, so where is the motive? I think the bank robbery is a coincidence."

"You could be right." Frank shifted to see her in the glow of the freeway lights. "But you've given us nothing to work with."

"What about whoever told that reporter I was missing?"

"I followed up on that, remember?" Carissa asked. "The reporter didn't know who he'd spoken with."

"You really believe that?"

"I don't have much choice. I can't compel him to give me information."

Katrina sighed. "This really stinks."

Her words echoed Frank's thoughts.

"Maybe one of us was the target." Marc glanced his direction.

"How do you figure?"

"I don't know. It's a stretch. But let's say the report about the gas leak was accurate. And then say the car we thought was headed for Katrina was simply a distracted driver who managed to avoid hitting her car at the last minute."

"The tracker was on my rig." Frank's stomach

sickened. "I was the one shot." The air in the SUV grew hot fast, and he felt lightheaded. He lowered the window. If Marc was correct, Frank was putting everyone around him in danger.

He had no idea what to think. He'd put enough criminals behind bars that it was entirely possible one had been released and had come after him.

11

Tuesday morning Katrina sat next to Frank's hospital bed. Her protection team stood outside the room talking in hushed tones with an FBI agent. She'd love to know what they were saying. She'd thought about Marc's theory all night long.

Had hearing that conversation in the breakroom and then having the explosion at her house really been a coincidence? It made sense. She and Frank had both jumped to the conclusion she was in danger without any real proof.

All of this could have literally been a series of unfortunate events leading to a huge coincidence.

Her thoughts drifted to the conversation she'd had with Frank about God. She wanted what he had. Even when he'd been shot, he hadn't freaked out or blamed God. He was definitely different than most of the people she'd met, and she suspected it had a lot to do with what he called his relationship with God.

Frank's eyes opened. He looked confused at first, but then his eyes cleared.

"Good morning," she said. "How are you feeling?"

"My shoulder hurts, but other than that, fine. What are you doing here?"

"Well that's a fine how do you do," she teased.

He winced. "Sorry. How are you?"

"Now you're repeating my questions back to me." She grinned. "To be honest, I'm rattled. The past few days are catching up to me."

"I understand. It's been pretty crazy."

"Yeah." She looked down and then back at him. "May I ask you a personal question?"

"Sure."

"The other day you said something that's stuck with me."

"Uh-oh."

"No uh-oh. It's about your relationship with God."

"Oh. What do you want to know?" His gaze rested on her face.

She caught her breath. Even with him in a hospital gown, she was drawn to him—big time. "How do you do it?" She shook her head. "I mean. I know about reading the Bible and going to church. I've done those things, but I don't have what you have. I want more."

"That's exactly how you do it. Your desire for more is going to grow your relationship with the Lord. Do you pray?"

She shrugged. "I prayed that night when my house exploded, and I was trapped."

"I think I might have too." His mouth tilted in a half-grin. "Start with talking to Him."

110

"How?"

"Like you talk to me. Tell Him how you feel. What your concerns are. Then just be quiet and wait."

She shook her head. "I don't know, Frank. I don't think I can do that."

"You don't have to talk out loud. Talk to Him in your head if speaking your thoughts feels too weird."

"Hmm. I could do that."

"Good. Let me know how it goes."

"I will. Thanks."

"Any time. Where are Marc and Carissa?"

She motioned toward the door. "Your FBI friend is with them."

Understanding filled his eyes. "Where'd everyone sleep last night? I don't recall anyone being here."

"You were out of it most of the night. Do you remember talking with me?" She, along with the team, had spent much of the night right here. Carissa had taken her over to her apartment earlier this morning to shower and change clothes while Marc stood watch over Frank. They'd grabbed breakfast on the way back to the hospital.

"I don't remember anything." He furrowed his brows and closed his eyes. "I hate not remembering. Did Special Agent Richards ever show up?"

"Yes. He's actually been here a couple of times. He's talking with Marc and Carissa right now."

"Wish I was privy to that conversation."

She chuckled.

"What's so funny?"

"I thought the same thing a few minutes ago."

He reached out his hand.

She wrapped her warm fingers around his cold ones. "You okay?"

"I'm great," he said drily.

"I'm sorry you were shot. Especially if I'm the cause. I imagine you rue the day I moved in across the street from you."

"Not at all. You've made my life more interesting."

"Ha. From what I've seen, the last thing you need is more interesting."

His thumb caressed the top of her hand. "As it happens, I like interesting very much. Though I don't normally get shot."

"Good to know. I'd hate to think this was a regular thing for you." She grinned. "I owe you my life."

He shook his head. "You don't owe me anything. We're friends, and friends watch out for each other."

"But most people don't take a bullet for their friends."

He chuckled. "True. But we still don't know if that bullet was intended for me or for you. Any idea if they've made progress with my past cases?"

"Sorry, no."

He gently squeezed her hand before pulling his away and tucking it under his blanket. "Would you mind telling my team I'm awake?"

"Sure." She stood and pulled open the door. "Frank is feeling left out in here."

Carissa grinned. "He's up. Good. Let's go grab some coffee while the men talk."

Katrina joined the woman who'd fast become a friend. "I'm surprised you're willing to drink hospital coffee."

"I never said we were getting it here. There's a Tully's a short walk away. I spotted it this morning."

"Oh. I realize you're the professional, but do you think it's safe for me to be walking in public until we know for sure who the target is? I know we're fine inside the hospital, but out there?" She shuddered.

"Kyle, I mean Special Agent Richards, has a tail on us to be safe." She looked over her shoulder and lowered her voice. "It's looking like Frank is the target."

"You're kidding." Katrina stopped and reached for Carissa's arm. "Is the FBI going to protect him?"

"Probably not, but I'm not sure yet what's going to happen. Turns out Kyle is as good a guy as Marc has claimed, so we'll see."

Katrina stuffed her hands into her coat pockets. "I changed my mind. I don't want coffee. To tell the truth, I don't even like coffee. I only tried what you made to be nice."

Carissa's lips formed an O. She looked past Katrina's shoulder and imperceptibly shook her head. "You said you liked my coffee."

"I did. Yours was the first. But that doesn't change the fact I don't want coffee. You can go without me. I'd like to go back to Frank's room and sit with him."

Carissa raised both hands palms out. "Okay. You win."

Compassion filled her new friend's face. "For what it's worth, I understand." She motioned toward Frank's room. The men were still inside with him. "It looks like they aren't ready for us yet."

A few minutes later, Katrina looked toward Frank's room and realized Marc and Special Agent Richards were watching them. She took a bracing breath and reminded herself they were the good guys, and there was no reason to feel afraid, but she couldn't stop the fear that consumed her all of a sudden.

"Knock. Knock." Katrina pushed open the door to Frank's room and walked inside. "How'd your talk go?"

"It was rather disturbing." With his good arm, he motioned toward the chair beside the bed. "Have a seat and keep me company. I did get a little good news."

"What's that?" She sat.

"Looks like I'll be released in a couple of hours since the bullet only grazed me."

"That's great!" She grinned, but on the inside, worry consumed her. Where would Frank go? Where would she go? Was it safe for him to go home? Clearly, the house in Warm Beach was out of the question. And wherever he went, he'd need someone watching his back since he couldn't very well take care of himself with his arm in a sling and stitches in his shoulder.

"What's the matter?" Frank's voice tore her from her thoughts.

She blinked. "What do you mean?"

"You looked far away there for a minute."

"Lost in thought I guess."

"About what?"

She shrugged. "It doesn't matter. I'm curious about something."

"Shoot." He winced. "Poor word choice."

She chuckled. "What made you leave being a cop and go into protecting people?"

He frowned and suddenly looked ten years older than he had moments ago. "It's a long story and not one I've ever shared."

"I have all day."

He sighed. "If I tell you, I don't want to hear about it from Marc or Carissa."

"They don't know?" This must be bigger than she'd imagined.

"No."

"Mums the word." She mimed zipping her lips and tossing the key over her shoulder.

"The last year I was on the force was a difficult one. A guy named Jimmy killed a teen girl. Her dad was a friend." With his good arm, he reached for the water bottle beside him and drank slowly as he blinked rapidly.

Katrina waited as he collected himself. This must still be painful if the king of tough guys was getting emotional.

Frank set the bottle down then cleared his throat. "Jimmy was as guilty as sin, but all we had was circumstantial evidence until my partner found something. It was exactly what we needed to get a warrant and bring Jimmy in."

Katrina stayed silent, waiting for him to continue.

He sighed. "After Jimmy was convicted to life in prison, I learned, Drake, my partner, had planted the evidence that was used to put Jimmy away."

She gasped. "Oh no. What'd you do?"

"The only thing my conscience would allow. I had unequivocal proof of what he'd done. As much as I wanted Jimmy to pay for the murder, he was locked up because of evidence Drake planted. After much soul searching and praying, I turned my partner in. He doesn't know I'm the one who ratted him out, but I think he strongly suspects it's me."

"Why's that?"

"When I confronted him, he admitted what he had done."

"Is there a chance anyone else would have known what he did?"

"It's possible, but not probable. It was a complete accident that I found out. Drake slipped up one night. Said something that tipped me off."

"Wow. Then what?"

"Then I went to I.A."

"Internal Affairs?" That must have been a horrible position to be in. No one wanted to rat out their partner. She wasn't a cop, but instinct told her there had to be some kind of code to keep quiet.

"Yes."

"Did Jimmy get released?"

"Unfortunately. He's been a free man for a while now, which makes me think the FBI theory is off base."

She shook her head. "What theory is that?"

"I assumed you knew. They believe Jimmy is out for revenge."

"But you didn't do anything wrong." Why would this Jimmy guy go after Frank if he was the one who provided information that got him released? Then again, he wouldn't know that.

"To his way of thinking, I'm one of the cops who put him away and planted evidence to do so."

"Are you sure he's the one who killed your friend's daughter?" she asked softly.

"As sure as I am of my age."

"How can you be so certain if you only had circumstantial evidence? Did you look at anyone else?"

He scowled. "Of course we did, but all the evidence pointed to Jimmy. He did it."

"And now he's walking the streets a free man."

"It stinks, doesn't it? You know what else? I hope it is him who shot at me. And I hope we can prove it. I'd like nothing better than to see him locked up for attempted murder. At least he'd do time for something."

"If it's not Jimmy like the FBI thinks, who else could be after you? Would Drake shoot at you? I mean you did throw him under the bus so to speak."

"I have a hard time believing he'd fall so far as to try to kill me. Sure, he was livid and lost his job over it. He'll never be a cop again, but murder? That's a stretch."

"Then who else would want you dead?"

"I've been involved in so many cases, I can't recall everyone who might have a vendetta against me. Jimmy's the FBI's prime person of interest. At the very least, they'll check his alibi for the time I was shot."

"What about the tracker found under your SUV? Any fingerprints?"

"Only mine and Marc's showed up when they pulled prints."

She sighed. They were getting nowhere. "I don't know how you do it. This is perfectly frustrating."

He chuckled. "I can't argue that. Enough talk about me. Tell me more about your ex-husband."

Her gaze slammed into his. She didn't like talking about that painful time in her life. "What do you want to know?"

"Why'd you divorce?"

"He was controlling and verbally abusive. As it turned out, my parents knew what they were talking about. They warned me, but I wouldn't listen."

"I'm sorry you had to go through that. What I don't understand, though, is why you didn't reconcile with them after you were no longer married."

"Easy. Stubborn pride." They knew she'd divorced, but it hadn't changed anything between them.

He winced. "It's not too late to pick up the phone."

"I tried that. They don't answer." Though if she were honest, her pride was part of the problem. "Why'd you want to know about Jason?"

"Guess I don't want to make the same mistakes he did. I do tend to be on the controlling side—a hazard of the job."

"I get that, but it's different with you. He had to know where I was at all times. If I was even five minutes late, he'd assume I was with another man."

"Wow."

"I know." She felt sorry for the new Mrs. Gibson. Hopefully, Jason had grown up and had a healthy self-esteem now. "Did anyone ever find out who called that reporter?"

"No, but we were able to determine it wasn't your ex. He didn't have a clue what was going on with you."

"Who spoke with him?"

"Marc took a drive yesterday to see him."

"He's a busy man."

"Come to think of it, he did have a pretty big day yesterday."

Frank's doctor breezed into the room. His height and Frank's were almost the same, and he wore his hair pulled back in a ponytail.

"I'll give you some privacy." Katrina stood and stepped into the hall. The FBI agent was still talking with Marc and Carissa. How had they not run out of things to say?

Marc spotted her first and waved her over to join them. "We were discussing where Frank should stay. We're taking him back to his home."

"Wouldn't that be the first place whoever is after him would go?"

The FBI man shook his head. "Not necessarily. If this is who we think, we suspect he happened across Frank by accident. Frank always parks inside his garage or the secure garage at his office. No one tampered with his vehicle at the lot, and the chances someone broke into his garage to place a tracker is illogical if the motive was to kill him. If he knew where he lived, why not take him out there?"

He asked a good question. "I see where you're going. So you think the tracker was a crime of opportunity?"

"Yes. Jimmy's last known address was in Seattle. Frank was parked in Seattle yesterday for several hours."

"Jimmy hasn't been questioned yet?" She would've thought the police or FBI would have interrogated the suspected murderer hours ago.

"He wasn't at his last known address. We're still quietly looking for him. We don't want him to spook and disappear."

The doctor left Frank's room and approached

them. "I'm discharging your friend now. A nurse will print off wound care instructions."

"What about stitch removal?" Carissa asked.

"He'll need to contact his primary care doctor for an appointment, and if he can't get in, he should come back here."

"Okay," Carissa said. "Thanks for everything."

"You're most welcome. Frank was a good patient."

Carissa chuckled. "Sorry, but that doesn't sound anything like Frank. Are you sure he's okay?"

The doctor grinned. "Yes. The bullet only grazed him. So long as he takes it easy and infection doesn't set in, he should recover nicely."

Katrina blew out a breath and grinned widely. "That's the best news I've heard in days."

Marc had a duffle bag over his shoulder. "Guess that's my cue to get in there. I ran by his place earlier and picked up clean clothes." He turned and headed for Frank's room.

Katrina met the gaze of the FBI agent. "Are you going to keep him safe?"

He frowned. "I'm only here as a friend. I wish there was something I could do officially, but Carissa and Marc know what they're doing. They'll make sure he stays alive."

"What about his old partner at the police department where he worked?"

"I was his partner," Carissa said.

"No, the other one."

Carissa tilted her head. "Drake? What about him?"

Uh-oh. She never should have brought the man up in front of Carissa. Somehow, she had to keep what happened out of this conversation. She didn't want to break Frank's trust. "Uh...maybe he has some idea who could be after Frank."

"Hmm. Good idea. I'll see if I can track him down," Carissa said. "I'm surprised none of us thought of that."

Special Agent Richards nodded. "May I have a private word with you?"

She glanced at Carissa who shrugged almost imperceptibly.

"Okay." She walked with the special agent about ten feet away.

"How'd you know he had a partner besides Carissa? I worked with them this past summer, and the only person he ever mentioned was Carissa."

She couldn't give away Frank's confidence. "Frank must've mentioned it. You know we're friends. We've had many talks over glasses of iced tea after he mows my lawn"

The strain in his eyes eased. "That makes sense."

"Mind if I ask you something?"

"You can ask, but I might not be able to answer."

"I understand." She laced her fingers together in front of her. "Frank told me that someone tipped off the FBI about the bank robbery yesterday. Do you know who?"

"I'm sorry, but I can't answer that question."

She sighed. "Okay. How about this one? Is it safe for me to go back to work at the bank? I mean, after all, I did tip you off about what I thought was a planning session for the same robbery, which was an inside job. What if more people there are involved that we realize?"

"We're looking into that theory, but the man who could have given us that information is dead."

"You sure he was the only on in the know? I realize you can't say so, but if you know who your tipster was, wouldn't it be possible he knows who all was involved?"

Special Agent Richardson pressed his lips together. Clearly, he wasn't going to answer.

"So should I go back to the bank or not?" She needed to work, but she could find another job. Besides that, she never wanted to step foot in that place again.

"I won't presume to know what's best for you, but I'd say go with your gut."

"Okay." Her gut said to stay as far away from the bank as possible, so that was exactly what she'd do. Frank trusted this man, so she would too. Now to figure out her next move.

12

Carissa snuggled into Marc's side at his apartment. A fire glowed in his gas fireplace, warming the small space.

"I think one of us should check on Katrina," Carissa said. After resuming a talk about their future plans, making a decision about their wedding, and then speaking with Katrina again about the sublet, she'd asked to see Marc's apartment. Marc had given her run of the place to see if she wanted to sublet it.

"Remind me why we decided to sublet your place and not mine?" Carissa asked. "You have a spare room and nicer finishes."

"But you have that balcony with a view that you enjoy so much."

"Good point." She'd miss the view if they were to move to Marc's place after they were married. There was nothing like sitting on the balcony gazing off into the distance at the lake.

"I try." He grinned. "Besides, you have more stuff than me so it's easier for me to move."

Carissa turned toward Marc. His brown eyes almost looked black as the fire played off his irises. His broad shoulders filled out the entire cushion behind him. He was even better looking to her today than the day they'd met. She was happy with the decision they'd made, but she wasn't sure how they'd pull it off.

His warm gaze caressed hers. "What're you thinking?"

"Only how incredibly good looking you are." Her face warmed.

"Hmm. I like the sound of that coming from your lips. I think the same way about you." He dropped a kiss on her forehead. "What are we going to do about Frank?"

"Way to kill the moment."

"Sorry. You're always Miss Business, but if you're not going to be, one of us needs to stay focused."

"Yeah. Yeah. I get it." She sat up and shifted to face him.

"What do you know about this Jimmy guy? Other than what Kyle already told me?"

"Only that he got off for a murder that Frank is certain he committed." It finally made sense why Frank had left the police force when he did. Why hadn't she thought of it sooner? He must have lost faith in the justice system.

"What are you thinking?" Marc asked.

"Nothing."

"You can't say that. I know you too well. You thought of something. What is it?"

"I need to talk to Frank."

"What about?"

"The past. Shortly after Jimmy's charges were reversed, Frank approached me about leaving the police force and going into business with him."

"You think they're connected?"

"I'm not sure. Maybe."

"Why were the charges dropped?"

"Evidence tampering." She didn't believe for one minute Frank would tamper with evidence to get his man, but that didn't mean Jimmy didn't believe it. If Jimmy was, indeed, after Frank, that was more than likely his motive.

"Frank tampered with evidence?"

Her eyes widened. "I can't believe you would even think that. You know Frank better than that."

"Desperate men have been known to do much worse. If he knew Jimmy had committed murder but lacked the evidence to prove it—"

"No!"

Katrina walked into the room. "Excuse me. I don't mean to interrupt, but I've seen all I need to see." She crossed her arms and shot daggers at Marc with her eyes. "I didn't mean to eavesdrop, but you made it difficult to not overhear. There is no way Frank would ever plant evidence."

"Thank you," Carissa said. "Finally, someone with some sense." She stood and turned her attention to Marc. "Speaking of Frank, let's go back to his place. I'm sure Kyle is wondering what's taking us so long. We were supposed to be here long enough for you to pack a few things and go."

"Which I did. Now we can go."

Marc stood and looked at Katrina. "What did you think of the apartment?"

"It's nice. Send me a contract, and I'll make my decision."

"Really?" His eyes widened.

"What?" Carissa asked. "You didn't expect her to like your place." She shook her head. "Then why even offer it?"

He shrugged. "I thought it was a long shot. She's used to a house. I figured she'd probably want to stick with one."

Clearly in a hurry to get back to Frank, Katrina led the way to the door. "I would prefer a house, but subletting is a great answer to my problem. I only need a place for a couple of months, tops. I could probably stay in an extended stay motel or short-term rental, but I think this helps us both."

"True." Marc grabbed his suitcase.

Carissa grinned. She liked Katrina. It was about time Frank found someone. Since Katrina would need to find a place to live sooner than later, Carissa would need to locate a wedding venue fast. That was the decision she and Marc had made together. She'd hoped to put it off and plan, but the challenge of planning a wedding in a little more than a week lit a fire in her. It might be fun to get married at Frank's house. They could decorate his backyard for the ceremony and the bare front room would make the perfect spot for the reception, sans the white carpet.

"You coming?" Marc looked over his shoulder at her.

"Right behind you." She pulled the door closed and double-timed it to catch up.

Frank shook his head. "No way. There is absolutely no way you can have a wedding here on New Year's Eve." Carissa had lost her mind if she thought getting married in his backyard in December was a good idea. Clearly, the woman hadn't looked at his backyard, much less taken the weather into consideration.

"Why not? Marc and I will do everything. You won't have to lift a finger. Not that you could anyway with your arm in a sling."

"How about you take a look in my backyard and save me the trouble of explaining."

Carissa huffed and marched to the slider. She flipped on the outside light then pulled the slider open and went outside. "Oh my. Frank what's wrong with you?" She stepped back inside looking like a kid who didn't get anything for Christmas. "It's all dirt and weeds."

"I'm aware. It's on my to-do list." The list that never got touched.

She sighed. "I thought if Marc and I ripped out the white carpet you hate so much in the front room and laid your flooring of choice, we'd be set, but that and the yard? There's no way. With Christmas this week, we won't be able to get the kind of help this place needs."

"And now you understand why I said no."

She nodded. With slumped shoulders, she plopped onto the carpeted floor near the recliner where he sat. "Maybe there's a way. If we keep the guest list small we could have it in your front room."

"What's the deal with having the wedding here? I thought you wanted a church wedding."

"That would be my first choice, but there's no way we'd be able to book a church for next week. Besides that, we need to watch your back, and we can't do that if we're visiting church venues." She sighed. "The only way a wedding will work in this time frame is to have it here. I figured I could get Katrina to bake the cake considering how much she enjoys baking. We could throw together some finger food and call it good."

Frank studied Carissa a moment. She'd been so excited when she was telling him about her plan for the wedding in his backyard. Maybe he could call in a favor or two. It was the wrong time of year to lay sod or plant grass though, so they'd have to come up with an alternative. "You know, this might not be as impossible as it seems."

She looked at him with speculation. "How? That yard is a completely blank slate. You don't even have a patio. How is that possible?"

"When I moved in there was a deck, but it was in bad shape and dangerous, so I tore it out."

"Looks like you tore more than that out."

He chuckled. "I did. Then work got busy, and I haven't had a breather to finish."

Marc trotted down the stairs. "Kyle called. They tracked Jimmy to Oregon."

Frank's fingers dug into the arm of the recliner. "And?"

"He has an alibi."

"Maybe he hired someone," Carissa offered.

"Not likely." If Jimmy hadn't shot at him, who had? He'd been so certain.

13

From the vantage point of the kitchen, Katrina observed Frank and Carissa. It was clear, at least to her, that Frank wanted to do everything he could to help Carissa, but given his current situation, there wasn't much he could manage. Considering everything they had done for her, the least she could do was volunteer her time. It wasn't like she was going to work this week.

Before she did anything though, she needed to call Rick. She still didn't like the man, but he deserved the courtesy of a phone call. She retreated to her bedroom upstairs and placed the call.

"This is Rick."

"Hi, it's Katrina. I wanted you to know that I won't be returning to work. After what happened, I don't feel comfortable being there. I'll make it official in writing but thought you should know right away."

He sighed. "I understand. How about you take some time to process everything. Enjoy Christmas and get back to me on Monday. If you still want to resign, I'll write you a letter of recommendation."

"You will?" She couldn't hide her surprise. She'd thought her boss didn't care for her.

"It would be my pleasure. I'm sorry about what happened yesterday. To be honest, I don't want to go back either."

"Really?"

"You sound surprised."

"I guess I thought nothing rattled you."

"I'm human, Katrina. It's not every day I experience a bank robbery and then have someone shot and killed in my place of employment. I'd have to be heartless to not feel the effects of something like that."

"I'm sorry. I know you're human and that had to be traumatic." She was still jittery from getting shot at last night, so she understood.

"I was actually planning to call all the employees to let everyone know the bank will be closed until Monday. But there was something else I needed to tell you."

"Oh?"

"Yes. Right after you left yesterday, one of the police officers gave me a note. It regards you and your friend. I'm sorry for opening it. I wasn't thinking and didn't notice your name on the front until after I'd already read it."

"That's fine." Katrina's stomach knotted. "What kind of note?"

"An unsettling one for sure. I was so flustered with all that had happened I stuffed it in my pocket and didn't read it until a short time ago."

"What did the note say?" She struggled to keep her tone friendly.

"It was quite unsettling."

"What did it say?" Her impatience came out in her tone. "This is very important."

"It said, 'You'd be wise to discontinue your association with Frank Davis. Your life could depend on it.' That's it word for word."

"Freaky."

"I thought so too. Are you in a safe place?"

"I think so." Her heart pounded. "Will you take a picture of that note and text it to me?"

"Of course. Are you in some kind of trouble, Katrina? It sounds like a jealous boyfriend."

"No boyfriend. May I send a friend to pick up the note from you?"

"I guess." He gave her his address.

"Thanks. A man named Marc or a woman named Carissa will be by this evening if that's okay."

"Sure. What's going on? You don't seem overly surprised by the note."

"Not much surprises me lately. But I wasn't expecting a message like that. I would still like the picture if you don't mind."

"I'll send it right now."

"Thanks."

"Sure. Stay safe and try to have a Merry Christmas, Katrina."

"I will. You too." She disconnected the call and

stared at her phone. "Who knew?" Her boss wasn't so bad after all. She left the room and bounded down the stairs. Her phone chimed indicating a text message.

"You guys need to see this. Rick received it yesterday and forgot to look at it until a little while ago"

Frank reached for her phone and frowned. "We need that note."

"I have his address. He said it's okay to come and get it." She looked at Marc and Carissa. "Who wants to go?"

"Send it to me." Marc stood and slipped into his coat. "I'll be back as soon as I can."

She glanced at Carissa whose gaze followed him to the door. "Why don't you go with him?"

"I can't leave Frank without protection, and now it looks like we're back to protecting you too."

"Wait a minute," Frank said. "I think it's clear I'm the target, and she's being warned to stay away from me or trouble will come to her too. Sounds like whoever is behind this is warning her off. But why?"

"No kidding," Carissa said. "Since when do the bad guys have a heart?"

"It's Christmas. Maybe it gave this one some compassion," Katrina said. "They are human." No matter how despicable or unfriendly a person came across, she believed most had a shred of decency in them. She assumed the person behind this warning was one of those who had a little goodness inside.

She told the team about the rest of her conversation

with her boss. "Which means, I'm unencumbered. I can help with your wedding plans."

Carissa shook her head. "I don't see how it will make much difference. The backyard will be too much work. It'll probably rain on us anyway if we hold it outside. Forget the wedding for now. This clue might be the lead we need."

She waved a hand. "There's no such thing as too much work. It's a blank slate. It so happens I'm good at this kind of thing. All we need are some pavers or artificial turf and something pretty that you can stand under to say your vows."

"You're not listening. I can't be bothered with wedding planning right now, and an outdoor wedding this time of year is a recipe for disaster."

Katrina widened her eyes. "What about a minister?"

Frank raised his chin. "I know a guy. He's on vacation through Christmas though."

Carissa looked his way. "Jenna's dad?"

"Yep."

Carissa's furrowed brow smoothed. "Great idea. But we still don't have time to plan a wedding."

Katrina waved a hand. "Leave it to me."

"Really?" Carissa asked. "That's a lot to do with so little time."

"I could use the distraction."

Carissa grinned. "Okay. Thanks. I'll text Peter and see if he'll ask if Jenna's dad is available. We can do a little ceremony inside someplace. So long as my parents can be there nothing else matters."

"Now hold on," Frank said. "Peter deserves a vacation without us pestering him. Trust me on this. It'll keep until Monday. In the meantime, I suggest the two of you brainstorm wedding locations." He leaned back in the recliner raising his feet higher. "I'm going to take a nap."

Carissa's eyes widened. "How can you rest after reading a note like that? We need to do something."

"There's nothing I can do at the moment. Marc has everything handled, and I'm tired." He folded his hands over his stomach and closed his eyes. "I can feel you gawking. Stop."

Katrina couldn't believe he was so calm. "But the note."

He opened one eye and looked at her. "Don't stress over that note. That message was more for me than you."

"You know who sent it?"

"I have a good idea. Now hush so I can think."

Carissa shot her a look then crossed her arms. "I thought you were going to sleep."

"Same diff."

Katrina stifled a chuckle. It was no laughing matter, but Frank had a way of lightening the mood, which she appreciated.

An hour later, Marc returned with the note. "I called Dillon. He's going to swing by soon."

Frank opened his eyes and sat up. "I didn't want to have this conversation, but I think it's necessary. Pay attention because I'm only saying this once."

"Why not wait for Dillon?" Carissa asked.

Frank sighed. "He doesn't need to know this, but you do." He went on to tell the same story he'd told Katrina about his former partner.

Katrina pressed her lips together, and her gaze darted from Carissa to Marc to see their reactions. Would they support his decision to report the evidence tampering or would they judge him harshly? They should support him since it was the right thing to do, but she still wondered.

"*You're* the one who turned in Drake?" Carissa paced the room then whirled on Frank. "Why didn't you say something sooner? All this time I've wondered."

Frank's face hardened. "Wondered what?"

"You left the P.D. so soon after all that went down. I couldn't accept you would stoop to planting evidence, and I knew Drake had been disciplined for it, but in the back of my mind…"

"You wondered how I couldn't have known since we were partners?"

"Exactly."

"For the record, I had nothing to do with it, but when I found out, I confronted Drake. He admitted what he'd done. I turned him in."

"But why? If Jimmy was guilty why not let it stand?"

"Because it wasn't right. That's not how the law works. We couldn't prove Jimmy was the killer."

"But you said—"

"I'm well aware of what I said, Carissa, but the truth is, I'm a rule follower. I can't stand by and knowingly allow a man to rot behind bars for life if we might be wrong. We never found enough evidence to convict."

"But your gut is never wrong." Carissa narrowed her arms.

"Not true. I've always wondered if Drake planted evidence to get an arrest on a few other cases." He blew out a breath. "Maybe I'll get a chance to find out. If I'm right and Drake is the person behind the warning to Katrina, then I'll be sure to ask him when we find him."

Unease consumed Katrina. It couldn't be a coincidence. "Uh, guys. I think I know Drake."

All three of their gazes shot her direction.

She licked her lips. "The security guard at the bank is named Drake. He also happened to not be at his post when I overheard the conversation in the breakroom."

Frank stood and planted a kiss on the top of her head. "Well done."

14

Frank didn't want Katrina anywhere near him if it would put her in danger. He had half a mind to send her away with Marc and Carissa to Oregon for Christmas. But he was in no position to be able to defend himself. Clearly, Drake was out for blood—his blood specifically.

A rap on the front door sounded in the quiet house.

"That's probably Dillon." Marc strode from the room. A moment later, he returned with the officer.

"I hear you found some more trouble," Dillon said.

"You could say that." Frank gave him the short version of his history with Drake.

Dillon ran his hand over his chin. "Do you have a plan?"

"Working on one." Definitely an overstatement, considering he had nothing.

"What do you have so far?" Dillon grabbed a barstool and brought it over to their group and sat.

"At the moment, nothing feasible," Frank said. "We

believe he's a guard at the bank where Katrina works."

"At least we know where to find him." Dillon said. "I could bring him in for questioning."

"On what grounds?" Frank asked. "We have nothing on him except for a note in his handwriting."

"That's enough," Carissa said. "Is that how you knew it was him? The handwriting?"

"Yes."

"The bank is closed until Monday," Katrina said.

"Then we won't be talking to him there." Dillon shifted on the stool. "We'll go to his home."

"Assuming he's there," Frank said. "He had to have known I'd recognize his handwriting. He's a smart man." He shook his head. "Though it pains me to admit it, Drake was always a half-step ahead of me."

"Let's assume he expected you to recognize the handwriting *if* you saw it." Carissa continued to pace. "If he and the security guard are one and the same, before yesterday, you'd never been to the bank, correct?"

Frank nodded. "So?"

"So, he took a risk writing that note by hand. He either wanted you to see it was him, or he actually doesn't want to hurt Katrina and tried to warn her away from you so she wouldn't get caught in the crossfire."

Marc shook his head. "No. If he was the one who shot at Frank, he would have seen Katrina."

"Not necessarily," Frank said. "She had her head down and was crouched in the middle of us. If we were doing our jobs right, he didn't see her."

Dillon thumbed the leg of the stool he sat on. "I think you could be right."

"Who's right?" Katrina asked.

"All of you. Well, all but Marc." Dillon shot Marc a weak grin. "We don't know if the shooter was Drake or not or if he did or didn't see you, but we believe at the least he didn't get a good enough look at you to identify you. If he knows you from the bank, he might sincerely not want to hurt you."

Frank followed Dillon's thought process and took it further. "Do we know who tipped off the FBI about the possible robbery?"

"No," Marc said. "But in light of this new information, I wonder if Kyle would be willing to share?" He pulled out his phone and typed a text into it. "Now we wait."

If Kyle confirmed Drake tipped them off, all the pieces would fit. Drake had probably been nearby to see what happened and spotted him outside the bank with Katrina. It all made sense.

Marc's phone chimed with an incoming text message. Marc frowned. "He confirmed it and wants to know what we know."

"Get him on the phone. This is the FBI's jurisdiction." As much as Frank would love to take down Drake himself and make a citizen's arrest, he didn't want to do anything that would compromise the case against his former partner.

Dillon regarded him with a curious gaze.

"What?" Frank asked.

"Did Drake have any special talents when he was on the force? Was he a sharpshooter?"

"No." But there was that time… His eyes widened and his feet plopped to the floor. "He has experience with bombs. Once when we were on a call, there wasn't time to wait for the bomb squad, and he was able to diffuse it." Frank focused on Katrina. "Was Drake at work the week your home exploded?"

She nodded. "Except for Friday. I didn't think anything of it though. Then yesterday when he wasn't there, I figured the FBI worked it out for him to be gone so they could insert their own guy into the part."

Frank stood. "People, I think we've figured this out. Marc, Kyle needs to be read in on what we know."

Marc held up his phone. "He's been on speaker. As soon as you told me to call him, I did."

"Hey, everyone," Kyle said. "Sit tight, and I'll get things moving on my end. I'll be in touch."

Marc looked at the screen. "He hung up."

Frank ran a palm down his jeans. "Now we wait." Kyle's lack of sharing information was annoying, but it was clear they'd struck on something important.

Dillon rubbed the back of his neck. "This doesn't feel right. It's too easy."

"Nothing wrong with easy," Carissa said. "Besides we've been trying to figure this out for days. It all finally clicked together.

A sound at the door drew their attention. Frank put

a finger to his lips then motioned for everyone to fan out.

The front door burst off its hinges and flew several feet into Frank's entryway. Frank ducked behind the kitchen wall.

"I know you're there, Frank." No way Frank could mistake that voice.

"I don't want anyone but you and Katrina."

"Leave her out of this." Frank motioned for Carissa to get Katrina out the slider.

Dillon and Marc moved into position at the end of the entryway just out of sight from Drake.

"Too late for that. That woman is a thorn in my side. Then again, were it not for her, I never would have spotted you outside the bank that day, so I owe her a thank you, which is why I decided to let her live after all. If only she would have stayed away from you. I warned her."

"A little late. She just got the message a short time ago. Besides, her house had a gas explosion. She needed a place to stay."

Drake laughed. "You actually bought the gas leak story? I thought you were smarter than that."

"What are you talking about?" He called 9-1-1 and spoke softly into his phone.

Footsteps sounded on the marble flooring. "I

figured she'd heard us talking about robbing the bank after I overheard Rick give her a hard time for not being at lunch. I couldn't risk she'd go to the authorities. I set a bomb in her garage to go off when I knew she'd be arriving home. The woman is predictable. Then she had to change things up that night. If she had parked in her garage like normal I would have succeeded. Thought at first I had, but then after my talk with that reporter I realized I'd failed."

"Are you the person who reported her missing?"

"You're off your game, Frank. Catch up. It was all me. I did a little digging and discovered she'd been married. Figured it would throw everyone off if I used her ex-husband's name."

Drake had that right. He needed to step up his game.

"I even snuck back onto her property after the fire department left to retrieve the bomb evidence. Carissa almost caught me, but I managed to slip away without notice."

"Everything was you?" It all fit now. "Why'd you tipped off the FBI?"

He shrugged. "I had to. My partner changed the plan. You know how I feel about that."

That explained his irrational behavior. Drake hated having a plan changed. "So you got angry and decided to turn on him."

"That's *your* specialty. You had no problem destroying my career."

"You did that to yourself." Where were the police? He really didn't want a shootout in his house. It was bad enough the front door had been blown off its hinges.

"I did what it took to put a killer behind bars."

"How did you sink so low? You're just as bad as Jimmy."

"Don't you say that! It's your fault. You caused this. Now you're gonna pay for everything."

"There's no way you're getting out of this, Drake. It's over. The police are on the way. My team has you in their sights." Okay, not exactly true, but a few steps closer and they would.

"You're not going to shoot me. Mr. Goody-Two-Shoes follows the rules. This is what's going to happen if you don't want your house destroyed. You and Katrina have exactly thirty seconds to show yourselves. If you don't, this entire place will blow." He chuckled. "Bet you didn't think I had it in me." Footsteps on the marble announced the man's departure. "I'll be waiting outside."

Frank's insides sank. *Lord, please protect us.* He stepped out from behind the wall with his good arm raised. "Katrina's gone." Out the side of his mouth he told Marc and Dillon to get out.

"Liar. I saw her come in."

"And I sent her out the back door as soon as you entered." Frank walked through the door opening. He prayed Marc and Dillon had escaped into the backyard and over the fence. Where were Carissa and Katrina?

145

Were they far enough away or hiding nearby and still in danger?

He walked closer to Drake who took several steps back.

"That's right. Keep coming." He stilled halfway down the driveway. "Stop." He raised his Glock and pointed it at Frank.

A shot ripped through the air. Frank winced. Wait—he hadn't been hit.

Drake fell to the ground, blood staining his shirt.

Frank looked to the left and spotted Dillon with his weapon drawn. The wail of sirens closed in. Frank blew out a breath. He rushed over to Drake and kicked the Glock out of his reach.

Drake looked up at him. "I hate you."

"The house didn't blow."

"There's no bomb. Figured you'd give up Katrina if you thought she was in danger." He winced. "Guess you were telling the truth."

"I don't lie." Frank almost felt sorry for the man. He glanced over at Marc who stood a few feet away with Dillon. "Call Kyle back."

"Will do." He had the phone to his ear.

"I still don't understand how you made the explosion at Katrina's look like an accident."

"I'm good."

Dillon approached the officers as they exited their vehicles. He clearly knew them. "We're going to need an ambulance."

Carissa and Katrina walked across the street from Katrina's home. His heart lurched at the sight of Katrina. Now that this was all over, he looked forward to getting to know her even more.

An ambulance drew to a stop behind the police cars. Once the medics were at Drake's side and attending to him, Frank got out of the way.

A short while later, Kyle arrived and parked nearby. He, along with several other FBI agents, approached the scene as Frank leaned against his house, waiting for the circus to end. His poor neighbors. When this was all over, he'd have to do something nice for them—mowing their lawns was out, but maybe he could talk Katrina into baking a bunch more Christmas cookies.

Kyle motioned Frank to join them.

Frank pushed off the wall and sauntered to the edge of the driveway. "Thanks for coming."

"I heard he blew your door off the hinges," Kyle said.

"Yep. You no sooner ended your call with us and the door went flying. I'm glad no one was in that part of the house. Drake also admitted to setting off a bomb in Katrina's garage and then removing the evidence."

Kyle blew out a long breath. "What a mess."

Dillon sidled up to them. "We got a name."

"Drake gave up the name of his third partner in crime?" Frank never expected him to snitch.

"He thought it might encourage the D.A. to show mercy on him and said something about a change in plans. Then he cussed me out for not killing him."

Frank frowned. He felt sorry for his old partner. He'd sunk lower than he thought possible.

Later that night, after Marc and Dillon had replaced his front door they all sat in his living room munching on cookies.

"I just realized we have the next week and a half off. We can get married next week and have Christmas with my parents." Carissa grinned.

Frank sighed. He enjoyed being with these people. If everything went back to the way it was supposed to be, he'd be alone again. Bah-hum-bug. "Or you could invite your parents here for Christmas."

Carissa laughed. "Uh...I don't think so. Have you seen your place? You have the most un-merry house on the block. Except for Katrina's." She looked at Katrina. "No offense."

"None taken."

"Why not come to Oregon with us? I'm sure you both could use a change in scenery."

"Go to Oregon?" Katrina asked.

"Sure. I'll run it by my mom, but I can't imagine she'd have an issue. She's been taking in strays my whole life."

Frank reached his good arm out and grasped Katrina's hand. "We've been delegated to strays. What do you say?"

Katrina wrinkled her nose.

He snort-laughed.

Her hand shot to her mouth.

Carissa chuckled. "You two talk and let me know. We're leaving in the morning, assuming the police are finished with us." She sucked in a breath. "Dillon. I didn't mean to leave you out. Do you have plans for Christmas?"

"I do. Thanks for the offer."

"Anytime."

Thank You, Lord, for this family You've given me. Katrina too. I don't know what the future holds for us, but I sense great things ahead. Also, thanks for having my back today when Drake was out for my blood.

Happiness and contentment flowed through him. He looked forward to what the New Year had for him and his team. He hoped and prayed it'd be much tamer than this past one.

Epilogue

New Year's Eve

Carissa couldn't believe they'd pulled it off—a New Year's Eve wedding at the home of a former client. The Drummond's cliffside estate in Lincoln City had been the farthest location from her mind. Out of the blue, Mrs. Drummond had phoned to see how she was doing. When Carissa had shared that they were hoping to get married on New Year's Eve but had yet to find a suitable location, she'd offered her home—the home where she and Marc worked their first case together and had fallen in love. Loved ones sat around them as they stood in front of a picture window that faced the Pacific Ocean.

Greenery with silver and white baubles decorated the space. Mrs. Drummond had hired a caterer as their wedding gift and allowed Katrina to use her kitchen to bake a cake.

Her parents sat front and center, beaming with happiness. Frank and Katrina sat beside them. Kyle had come along to be Marc's best man. She had decided against having an attendant since Frank was her best friend and it felt weird asking him. Pastor Walsh, Jenna's dad, had happily agreed to perform their ceremony. Peter and Jenna sat shoulder to shoulder, holding hands. Carissa noted the diamond on her left ring finger. She was happy for her colleague and his fiancée. To her knowledge, no date had been set. Sally, the final member of the Protection Inc. team, couldn't make the journey from Seattle, because she'd had her own excitement over their break. She's adopted a little girl. Carissa had no idea she'd been trying to adopt for years. She couldn't wait to meet the toddler. Things were definitely changing for the Protection Inc. team— good changes.

Pastor Walsh cleared his voice. "We are gathered here today in the presence of family and friends to celebrate the joining of two lives."

Carissa gazed into Marc's shimmering eyes. If someone had told her a year ago she'd be married to the man of her dreams before the New Year she'd never have believed them. Marc had once pointed out that the Lord delighted in seeing her happy. Well, He must be quite happy right now.

She looked forward to their next adventures as husband and wife, but for now, she would bask in the moment. She refocused her attention on Pastor Walsh as they repeated their vows.

"You may seal the deal with a kiss." Pastor Walsh grinned.

Everyone laughed.

Marc pulled her close and pressed his lips to hers in a toe-tingling kiss.

Author Notes

I hope you enjoyed *Certain Threat*. It was a fun story to write. I especially enjoyed drawing from a past experience in this book. Back when my husband and I were in college he took a position as a youth pastor at a church in Warm Beach. A couple of my critique partners thought I made the place up, so I wanted to state here, that it's a real place.

It was quite a drive from Kirkland so we'd spend the entire day up there on Sundays. During the afternoons we often would either do something with the youth or go to lunch at the home of someone from the church. One of my favorite things to do there was go to a park set along the Sound. The whales swam so close to the shoreline. It was quite a sight to see!

I hope you found the ending to be satisfying. I do have at least two more stories in me, but I'm not certain when I'll be able to write them.

If you enjoyed *Certain Threat* I would be grateful if you'd leave a review for it.

I realize writing a review can be intimidating. All that is needed is a sentence or two about why you like the story. There is no need to summarize the story.

You can find me in the usual places online: Facebook, Twitter, and Instagram. There are easy links to all my social media on my website www.kimberlyrjohnson.com. Instagram is a new favorite site for me. I used to never take pictures but this past spring and summer I've been keeping a watch out for flowers, while I take long walks. It's been so fun! I try to post there every day. I'm not as faithful on other sites.

Thank you for your support. If you want to make sure you don't miss any of my books please subscribe to my newsletter. That can be done from the link to my website. I generally send out one newsletter a month to share about books sales, new covers, and new releases. Some months you will hear from me more, other months I'll be quiet. It really depends on what is going on in my life.

Be sure turn the page to discover more of my books. About half have some kind of mystery and/or suspense and the other half are contemporary romance.

Blessings,
Kimberly Rose Johnson

More Books by Kimberly Rose Johnson

Protection Inc.
Direct Threat
Imminent Threat
Certain Threat

Law Enforcement Heroes
Edge of Truth

The Librarian Sleuth
The Sleuth's Miscalculation
The Sleuth's Dilemma
The Sleuth's Conundrum
The Sleuth's Surprise

Brides of Seattle
Until I Met You
The Reluctant Groom
Simply Smitten

Melodies of Love
A Love Song for Kayla
An Encore for Estelle
A Waltz for Amber

Sunriver Dreams
A Love to Treasure
A Christmas Homecoming
Designing Love

Wildflower B&B Romance Series
Island Refuge
Island Dreams
Island Christmas
Island Hope

Contemporary Novellas
Brewed with Love
Sara's Gift